WHITEY AND THE SIX DWARFS

WINDY MOUNTAIN

BOOK 3

JOHN MARTIN

CONTENTS

This novel uses English spelling and grammar, with a sprinkling of Australian lingo.

ONE

SUSPICIOUS MINDS

KATY RAISED her head from the computer screen when she heard tapping on the front window.

It was Sergeant Stretch! Why was he here at this time of the morning?

Katy hadn't even had time to clear away yesterday afternoon's six empty cups, let alone open up the museum.

She went to the door, and let the policeman in.

He just grunted and walked past her to the counter, where he laid down his cap. He turned around, folded his arms, and leaned back so he could pan the foyer with squinty eyes as if he was going to stride over to one of the dirty cups and issue it with a defect notice.

He made a clicking noise with his tongue. "I hope you know what you are taking on, little lady?" Then he breathed out loudly. "I'm actually here on official business."

Katy rolled her eyes. "What's Moose supposed to have done now?" She had cut Stretch's hair for twenty years, so she was well aware of the bad blood between him and Moose. Moose was a man mountain who quite literally was the state's biggest expert on the Tasmanian Tiger, but he had also done some time in jail where his size had been both an asset and a curse. He had been so happy yesterday to finally get his plaster cast off and walk without the aid of crutches. This was going to turn his mood south again.

"Not him, *this time!*" Stretch ran a hand through his hair, which was longer than usual. "I was hoping to get some background information on the old couple who moved into Messerschmitt's old place in Hill Street. Mr and Mrs le Blanc? Know them?"

"Should I?"

"I thought you might have cut their hair."

"No, I haven't. Have you asked Vicki or Velda?"

Stretch gave the smallest of head shakes as he reached into his pocket and pulled out a roll of peppermints. "Messerschmitt never actually owned the house. It was rented out to him by you know who. When he did a runner, she had the place cleared out so it could go back on the rental market."

"What has the old couple done?" Katy asked.

Stretch unwrapped the mints and offered her one. The strong smell, mingled with the scent of his cheap aftershave, made her gag and she waved the offer away.

He kept holding out the roll. "Sure? Are you feeling all right? You look a bit pale."

He popped a mint into his mouth and started aggressively sucking it before locking eyes with Katy again. "This is just between you and I, right? It's not what the old couple have done. Quite the reverse. Someone has kidnapped one of the concrete dwarfs from their garden."

"Kids playing a prank?"

"That was my first thought," he said in a stream of minty breath. "But would kids go to the trouble of leaving a handwritten ransom note? Do children even get taught Cord Cursive any more?"

"Perhaps the kidnapper thinks Messerschmitt still lives there?" Katy said.

Stretch started crunching the mint as he considered this. "Unlikely," he said when he had swallowed. "Messerschmitt's dog kept a nicer garden than him. At least Adolf dug some holes."

Stretch's voice became more relaxed — less formal. "Heard from the old blokes?"

Katy pointed to the computer on the other side of the grey, laminated counter. "The email I just got from them said they were about to pick up a hire car to drive from Dublin to Donegal."

Stretch clicked his tongue again. "I don't envy the Irish traffic police. I presume Oodles is driving?"

Katy looked up at him. "Wish-Wash has never had a licence, and no one around here can remember the Mayor driving."

"Oh, I bet Moose can. Sergeant Smith was dead-set certain it was him who slashed the Mayor's tyres all those years ago. He just couldn't prove it."

James Northan, a.k.a. the Mayor, hadn't actually been the Mayor for some time but he was descended from Colonel Richard Northan, whose forebears had dominated the office since he founded the town in 1841. The mayoral chains now hung around the neck of James's daughter Maddie. She also headed the family trust that owned half the real estate in town, including the hairdressing salon she had just bought from Katy for her adopted daughters.

Stretch turned his head when he heard vehicles pulling up outside. The pitch of his voice rose as he slipped back into officious mode. "Are those tradies from the building site next door parking their utes in your car park? Want me to go tell them to move?"

"They're not harming anyone," Katy said. "They make the museum look busier than it is."

"Someone has to tell them they're trespassing." He was halfway to the door when the rungs on the staircase at the back of the room began reverberating.

Stretch looked around to see Moose limping down the final steps, scratching the hairy belly behind his unbuttoned shirt.

The bearded man locked eyes with Stretch.

"Nice bald spot you've got going there, Sergeant," Moose said.

Stretch looked like a tomato in a stiff blue uniform as he returned to collect his cap, which he slammed on his head before turning. "Some of us have proper work to do." He banged the glass door behind him.

———

Katy watched through the window as Stretch went straight past the building site and marched up the High Street.

"Did you have to tease him like that, Moose? He's sensitive about his bald spot."

"Is he, Kazza?" Moose laughed, then his face grew serious. "When we heard his voice at the top of the stairs we wondered what he was doing here."

"We?"

Moose turned around and shouted. "You can come down now, Awesome Sauce."

The Texan teenager came tiptoeing down. "Has he gone?" he said as he made it to the bottom and looked around nervously. The patchy growth on his face helped make him look like a scared little animal.

Katy put her hands on her hips. "Why were you hiding up there, Tim?"

"You don't know what it's like!" His voice went up and down. "Officer Stretch has inspected my visa, like, five or six times already but it hasn't stopped him demanding to see it again."

Moose glared at him. "You'd better hope Stretch doesn't get to hear about what you did to the mirror. He'd throw you in a detention centre for sure."

Tim looked wounded. "I said I was sorry."

"That mirror was legendary around here. Now it's in a million little pieces, and I'm not certain you've found them all."

"You were the one who asked me to remove it."

"Ever hear of a screwdriver? You only had to fucking ask."

"Moose! Language!" Katy looked from face to face. "Well, you both can breathe easy. Stretch says he only came here to gather information on the old couple who have moved into Messerschmitt's house. The le Blancs? Someone's kidnapped one of the ornamental dwarfs in their garden."

Moose pulled a face. "Stretch thinks I stole it?"

"You didn't listen to me. He was trying to put together a jigsaw. Did you know the property is owned by the Northans?"

Moose grunted. "Figures! I don't know what got into Oodles and Wish-Wash deciding to take the Mayor with them? Neither of them have the strength to push him out of a little window 35,000 feet above the Atlantic."

Katy rolled her eyes. "For your information, the Mayor got off the plane through the door with all the other passengers. I got an email from the old blokes earlier saying they had arrived safely in Dublin."

"They sent an email on their own?" Tim's eyes widened.

"I have been giving Wish-Wash some lessons. But now I think about it I'm guessing the Mayor must have sent this one. It was all in capitals. Even 11,000 miles away, he's still shouting at us."

"How long is the drive to Donegal?" Moose said.

Katy stared into space. "Three hours, I think. Joffa would know better."

Moose looked left and right. "Where is the Irish git?"

Katy sighed again. "Around the back."

"I'd better get out there before he catches another Native Cat."

Tim pinched the bridge of his nose. "You're never going to let us forget that!"

"Nonsense! Now I'm fit for real work again …"

"Whoa," Katy said. "Have you even got the medical all-clear?"

Moose kicked up his leg and rotated his foot. "They've removed the plaster. What more proof do you need?"

"A doctor's certificate maybe?"

"Who from? Every time I go up to the hospital I see a different Indian doctor. I think they've got an exchange program going with a takeaway."

Katy rolled her eyes again. "Go see Doc Jenkins. That's who I go to."

Moose prodded a finger on Tim's chest. "I don't need a poxy doctor to tell me I'm feeling fine. My return to health just means *you're* back in your proper place making tea and coffee for the customers on your fucking own."

He headed for the door.

Tim look relieved to see it close behind him, and watched him disappear around the side.

"What time is it?" he said.

Katy looked at her watch. "Goodness, the first tour bus will be here soon."

TWO
ALL SHOOK UP

TIM DISAPPEARED into the washroom to fill the urn, and Katy picked up the phone.

"I'm just feeling a bit under the weather," Katy told Yvonne, the doctor's receptionist. "I was hoping you could fit me in later today. Four o'clock? Okey dokey. See you then."

When she hung up, she looked around the room and realised she didn't even have the energy to help Tim straighten the chairs and collect the cups.

Perhaps Stretch was right? Perhaps she had bitten off more than she could chew?

What were Oodles and Wish-Wash even thinking when they handed over the ownership of the Windy Mountain Tasmanian Tiger Museum to her, Joffa and Moose? The only thing she knew about this carnivorous marsupial was that its extinct status was questionable.

She had never expected to do anything else but cut hair, style hair, perm hair and dye hair. And cut beards on the side. But no matter how drained she felt right now, there was no going back. She had sold the salon to Maddie Northan, who wanted to set up Vicki and Velda as hairdressers and didn't seem to care what the more conservative section of the community felt about the adopted Korean twins with their orange hair and nose rings. Stretch obviously hadn't built up the courage to entrust his head to them, so it was obvious why they hadn't been his first point of call to garner info about the le Blancs.

Katy still owned the flat above the business but instead of going downstairs to work each day, she now strolled to the museum on the outskirts of town. The 10-minute walk gave her and hubby Joffa an extra chance to chat. This morning he had gone straight to the shed and hadn't reappeared.

The museum was still getting three coaches each day, but the buses had fewer and fewer people on them.

That was probably a result of the bad publicity that came after the museum's latest public relations disaster.

No one was really to blame. It wasn't Moose's fault he had tripped over a branch and broken his ankle. And to their credit, Joffa and Tim had readily agreed to step up despite, in Moose's words, neither knowing their arses from their elbows.

The media had been enraged when Wish-Wash yanked off the covering on a cage, revealing something other than the promised Tasmanian Tiger.

No matter that the Irishman and American made the actual mistake, it was Oodles and Wish-Wash who copped it in the neck for weeks.

Who could blame them for wanting to just sell up? But who could blame people for not wanting to buy a tarnished business?

Oodles and Wish-Wash were between a rock and a hard place. Trying to tough it out wasn't even an option because they already had their trip to Ireland planned and paid for, and sensed if they put up a 'temporarily closed' sign, it would be seen as the first indication of surrender.

Instead, they signed the museum over to Katy, Joffa and Moose, and took the Mayor to Ireland with them.

How on earth would she manage on her own now Moose was fit for active duty again and intern Tim was due to go home soon?

Katy's thoughts were broken when Tim re-emerged from the wash-room and he saw the look on her face.

He was puffing as he wrestled the urn across the room, and looked relieved to put it down. "Are you all right, Miss Kate? You don't look well."

Katy took some deep breaths. "I'll be fine in a minute." He didn't need to know that was a lie.

————

Moose heard the loud music as soon as he started walking down the side of the museum. He looked over the fence and could see had a dozen workmen wearing brightly coloured hard-hats. They were all wearing hearing-protection gear, too, which explained why they had the radio turned up so loud. How could anyone be expected to concentrate with the noise of power drills and saws, nail guns, and what passed as music these days?

He found the Irishman around the back. Joffa was a younger version of himself. Both men were 6 foot 6, and 18 stone, with a bit of jail time in their pasts, but differentiated by a few grey hairs in Moose's beard and their differing accents.

"There you are?" Moose growled when he saw Joffa was not working but bending down and patting the dog Oodles and Wish-Wash had left in their care. "You just missed Sergeant Stretch."

"You think I didn't see him?" Joffa smiled as he looked up. "That's why I stayed out here." Gough rolled on to his back, and Joffa gave the dog a tummy rub. "What did he want?"

"He wanted to know if anyone knew about the old couple who have moved into Messerschmitt's old digs."

Joffa stood up. "What's Stretch think they've done?"

"It's what someone has done to them. They've stolen one of the concrete dwarfs from their garden."

"Which one?" Joffa said.

"How would I know?"

"He must have said."

"I didn't hear it," Moose said. "Does it matter?"

"If I knew which one, I could look out for it."

"Right! You know them all by sight do you?"

"I had to learn someting all those years locked up. Didn't you?"

Moose prodded his own chest. "I came out as a fully qualified brickie's labourer, mate."

"Last I heard, they don't ask a lot of questions at trivia nights about bricks. Not like, say, a question about which of the seven dwarfs doesn't have a beard."

Moose glared at him. "If you know so much about the dwarfs, go ahead and name them."

"Which ones? The originals penned by the Brothers Grimm didn't even have names. What are you even doing out here anyway? I thought you were still on light duties?"

"Not you, too?" Moose screwed up his face and kicked up his left leg again. "See, full movement. I'm almost ready to go bush again."

A vehicle crackling the gravel at the front of the building made Moose turn, then he laughed. "Time for Awesome Sauce to juggle 30 cups and saucers. If I wasn't so busy, I'd go give him a hand."

He went to investigate the new arrival. Even with a slight hobble, he had a spring in his step.

But he felt pale when he returned just seconds later. "You're not going to believe this. It's a fucking mini-bus!"

———

Joffa slumped into one of the plastic chairs outside the shed. "It's all my fault."

"I can't argue with that." Moose pointed to the museum wall. "But I do think that American twerp deserves at least half of the blame."

"We honestly thought that was a Tasmanian Tiger we had caught."

Moose sat down next to him. "Easy mistake to make. Stripes. Spots. They can be very confusing."

"Don't take the mickey out of me. I was behind that desk when the tour company offered to send three buses here every day. But they never promised how big those buses would be."

"Christ! Why didn't you sign a contract with them?"

"At the time, I was happy to get anyone to visit."

Moose pointed towards the car park. "That little bus would be lucky to carry eight people. Even if we get three mini-buses a day the takings won't pay everyone's wages, the tea and coffee we serve and the upkeep of the museum. For fuck's sake!"

Gough began whining.

Joffa stood back up and leant down to scratch the dog behind the ears.

"Maybe we both need a walk to clear our heads," the Irishman said. "With any luck, we'll find a cliff to walk off. I should never have let Katy sell the salon."

Moose sighed as he rose. "C'mon, let's go see Kazza before you go on your suicide walk."

Joffa looked like he had chewed on a lemon. "Her name's Katy. I don't understand how you can mangle that to 'Kazza'?"

"She answers to it, doesn't she? It's a good thing someone else around here understands Ockerisms. More importantly, she can tell us what the damage is with the mini-bus, so you can die more unhappily."

———

They saw the back end of red-checked trousers as soon as they went through the door. Then a striped blue and white shirt, and a green baseball cap.

It looked like Wish-Wash was leaning on the counter talking to Katy.

How could that be?

It became clear when he turned around. This man was as tall as Wish-Wash and his nose sloped the same way. But he was slimmer and much, much younger.

Wish-Wash's grandson! Moose had seen him a couple of days before when he had driven the three old blokes to the airport in his dual-cab ute, but he hadn't expected to see him again until the return trip. What was he doing back here? Moose looked around but the only vehicles he saw in the car park were battered tradies' utes and the lone mini-bus. "Where are your wheels, Rod?"

"You're looking at them."

"You're driving the mini-bus!"

Rod Whish-Willson nodded. "I parted company with the travel agent in Slutz Plains. Now I'm driving for Sally Hopkins's tour company."

Moose's eyes widened. "I thought the plan was for your grandfather to move in with you in Slutz Plains when he comes back."

'Yesssssss." Rod said slowly. "But I'm afraid this job required me to move to Launceston."

"Christ! You haven't told him, have you?"

"I haven't had a chance."

Moose felt the blood rising to his face. "Just how long have you known?"

"I didn't want him to fret about it on the plane all the way to Ireland. He was nervous enough as it was."

"When were you planning on telling him then?"

"When do you think the best time is? When he comes home?"

"Are you kidding me!"

"If you get to speak to him first, reassure him I have a spare room in my new digs."

"You want me to tell him!"

Rod scratched his head. "I can't think what the alternative is."

Moose looked at Joffa. What was going through his mind was the thought: do you want hit him or should I? But Joffa went off on a tangent. "Does Sally know what you are wearing, Rod?"

Rod looked downwards. "My uniform hasn't arrived yet. You don't think I'm overdressed?"

Moose rolled his eyes. "If the bus-driving doesn't work out, you could always get a job as a fucking colour-chart in a paint shop?"

Katy glared at him.

"What? I'm sure Rod doesn't mind a bit of feedback. I'm sure he's already taken a barrage about his dress sense from his customers."

"Actually no," Rod said. "He didn't speak a word to me on the whole trip."

Now Joffa saw red. "You don't mean to tell us you only had one person on the bus?"

Joffa looked searchingly at Katy sitting behind the desk, and she nodded, which made the bulging vein in his neck look like a matching pair for Moose's.

"Fair go," Rod said. "It's not like they let us stop at bus stops and pick up customers. I had one passenger at the depot — and I got him here safely. I wrote Katy a cheque for $19 so he could go in, and I was about to follow him in myself when you two blokes turned up."

Moose opened his mouth to speak but Katy got in first. "Haven't you two got things to do out back? BECAUSE neither of you is helping."

"We thought you might need a hand making the tea and coffees," Joffa muttered.

Katy's body language indicated she didn't believe a word of that. "I think I can manage."

Moose looked left and right. "I thought brew-making was Awesome Sauce's job? What have you done with him? Please tell me he's upstairs looking for more pieces of broken mirror."

"Will you lay off that boy, Moose!" Katy said. "If you must know, Tim has gone up to Hill Street to have a look around."

"Hill Street?"

"He's checking out the le Blancs' garden."

"Jesus, Kazza! Haven't we got enough going on — or not going on?"

Rod looked from face to face. "I think this is a good time for me to check out the gallery. That OK?"

Katy exhaled from her nose, and pointed to the entrance. "Be our guest."

Rod started walking across the foyer, but stopped and turned. "If it's not too much trouble, I wouldn't mind a biscuit with my tea when I come out."

———

They watched Rod disappear through the door. When it had finished swinging, Moose said, "Wish-Wash will never be dead while his grandson is around."

"That's a terrible thing to say." Katy stood up from behind the computer and put her hands on her hips. "I really don't think Wish-Wash will be leaving us any time soon."

"If he comes back from Ireland and finds he now has nowhere to live and, worse, the culprit has eaten all his chocolate digestives, he might have a fatal heart attack sooner than you think," Moose said.

"If that happens we'll have a ready-made replacement. Wash-Wish!"

Katy waggled a finger in the space between them. "Don't even joke about this, guys. We don't even know what type of biscuits he likes."

Moose turned to Joffa. "Care to make a bet? Loser has to carry all those books downstairs."

Katy frowned. "What books?"

"The ones in the upstairs sitting room."

"Wish-Wash's books?"

"Fucked if I know," Moose said. "They might have been here when he moved into the flat."

Joffa raised his hand. "Um, you can't throw out those books!"

"Why not? Wish-Wash left the museum to us. If he really wanted them, he would have made arrangements for them."

"Like where? You heard Wash-Wish. Wish-Wash now doesn't even have a home to go to."

"He'll thank us for doing him a favour then."

"Shouldn't you wait until he comes back?" Joffa said.

"Why do you even care?" Moose said.

Joffa folded his arms, looked to Katy for support, and sighed. "I suppose I'd better come clean. Those books never did belong to Wish-Wash." He exhaled loudly again. "I think he's been looking after them for someone else."

"You think?" Moose looked him in the eye. "You know who really owns them, don't you?" Then he turned his accusing eyes on Katy.

"Don't look at me," Katy said. "I didn't even know there were books up there until just now."

Joffa shielded his mouth with his fingers. "I'm sworn to secrecy," he mumbled.

"So you do know who owns them?" Moose looked daggers at him. "I thought we were supposed to be partners?"

Joffa looked Moose in the eye as he weighed the situation up. "You have to promise not to tell."

"For fuck's sake, we're not all kids."

"Swear!"

Moose spat into his palm and shook Joffa's hand. "I swear, all right. Happy?"

"They're Dave Jenkins's." Joffa looked from face to face."

Moose glanced at Katy. "Not your friend the doctor again?"

"Not him," Joffa said. "Dave is the undertaker. The doctor is his father." He looked to Katy. "Do you know the doctor's first name?"

"Jerry," she said.

Moose looked even more startled. "Jerry Jenkins! Here?"

"I thought you didn't know him?" Katy said.

Moose chewed on his bottom lip. "Who said I know him?"

"You sounded like you did."

"I was just caught by surprise, that's all. It's a funny sounding name isn't it? You'd call a mouse Jerry, not a doctor. And his son is the undertaker! Is that even legal?"

The three of them looked across the foyer when the front door crashed open.

———

"I've just seen a Tasmanian Tiger," Tim gasped as he approached the desk. He was dripping with sweat.

Moose looked at Joffa. "Here we go again!" He looked back to Awesome Sauce. "Were there pixies at the bottom of the garden, too?"

Tim studied Moose's face. "How did you know?" Then he started to sway.

Katy reached over the counter in an attempt to stop him falling over. "Grab him someone."

Joffa grabbed him by the armpits, and Katy handed over her metal water bottle.

Tim took a long swig. "Thanks, Miss Kate, I needed that. It's getting hotter than Hades out there."

"In your own time," Katy said. "Tell us what you saw?"

Tim took another swig and swallowed. "I saw it clear as day, I really did. It was standing in the le Blancs' garden still as a statue."

"Did it make any kind of noise?" Joffa asked.

"Not that I could hear. But it looked me right in the eye. When I finally unfroze, I hightailed it back here as fast as I could."

Moose was grumbling when he hobbled towards the door. "I'm on it, but there's going to be hell to pay if it's a fucking joke."

No sooner had he slammed the door behind him, they heard the gallery door swing open.

"Is the tea ready?" Rod asked as they crossed the room. "We're parched, aren't we Mr Sin?"

The squat bald-headed man with him just nodded.

He was short and wide — not fat, just a roundish ball of muscle with a long black beard.

Katy headed to the gate in the counter. "I thought you'd be in there longer than two minutes, Rod."

"I'm sure glad I didn't fork out good money to see that."

"You didn't read all the articles?" Katy asked.

"People of my generation don't want to be bogged down in written detail. We like more visual cues."

Katy bit her bottom lip. "Sorry you feel that way. I'll make the tea now. Tea bag all right? Or do want something more fancy smantzy. Ginger perhaps? Never can tell with you millennials."

She nearly choked when he said, "No, normal tea's fine — with a chocolate digestive if you've got one."

———

Twenty minutes later they were standing around in the foyer sipping tea.

All Mr Sin did was smile, nod and shake his head, which led Katy to think he might be mute.

When she heard footsteps crunching in the gravel car park, she looked out the window and saw Moose dragging his left foot as he approached the door.

He pushed open the door so hard, it's a wonder it didn't fly off its hinges.

He went straight to Tim and poked him on the chest. "I've got a bone to pick with you, Awesome Sauce. Those pixies at the bottom of the garden are actually garden gnomes. Concrete dwarfs. And the reason that Tasmanian Tiger was as still as a statue is it *is* a fucking statue!"

———

"I don't get it, Kazza." Moose turned on her. "This museum is on life support and you're sending this boy scout to case garden ornaments!"

"Now hang on." Joffa glared at Moose. "Katy didn't mean any harm to this museum."

Moose glared back. "Are you still here? I thought you were going out to top yourself."

Tim broke out of his stunned silence. "Are you trying to tell me that

Tasmanian Tiger wasn't real? We had a staring contest. It had beady little eyes and very realistic fur."

Moose glared at him. "Weren't you listening to me?" He prodded him on the chest again. "IT *IS* A STATUE! It's even dumber than you are!"

"What's it doing in a garden then?"

"How do I know?"

"Aren't you curious?"

Moose turned his head again when Katy spoke. "Tim has a point. This might be evidence that somehow ties into the kidnapping of the dwarf, don't you think?"

Moose threw his head skywards. "For fuck's sake, how? Anyway, since when did we join the police force?"

"What's wrong with being good citizens?" Joffa said.

"I don't believe it!" Moose's eyes bore into Joffa's. "Is this the same scaredy cat who was hiding from Stretch earlier? Now he wants to be a good citizen? Fuck me!"

Katy sighed. "Do you really have to swear in front of guests, Moose?"

He looked right back at her. "You wouldn't believe how restrained I'm being."

"You don't mind if I look into it a bit deeper," Katy said. "I get that you want me to concentrate on the well-being of the museum, but doesn't this new information bring this into our sphere? I mean it *is* a Tasmanian Tiger statue and we do have the only Tasmanian Tiger museum in town."

Moose folded his arms. "You haven't heard a word I've said, have you, Kazza?"

Moose turned to Rod. "No one else seems to get it. If your fucking tour company can only manage to send us three mini-buses each day we're not going to get enough people through here to be able to stay afloat. And that's even if the mini-buses are full. God help us if each one carries only one customer." He turned back to Katy. "And God help us even more if Wash-Wish here eats and drinks all our slim profits each day."

"What did you call me?" Rod said.

"Don't you listen to him, Rod." Katy said.

"Don't molly-coddle the boy, Kazza. He's getting off lightly. Remember what his father was like? Washed-up AND a Fuck-Up!"

"Don't be so insensitive!"

"Insensitive? My arse!" Moose said. "The kid didn't even know Billy Gumboots." He eyeballed him again. "Did you? You probably only went to his funeral to make sure your old man was really dead this time."

"Can I ask something?"

All eyes turned towards Mr Sin, who was still holding his cup and saucer. "Is this a good time to ask if this museum is for sale?"

THREE
HOUND DOG

MOOSE HELD Sin's business card in his hand as they stood on the footpath and watched the mini-bus become smaller and smaller as it drove away.

"What do you make of that?" Joffa blew out his cheeks.

Moose kept examining the card, and he broke into a grin. "I think we've fallen on our feet."

Joffa glared at him. "You really think the museum is ours to sell?"

"Sure I do. Oodles and Wish-Wash gave it to us."

"I can't believe you're even thinking that way, Moose?" Katy said. "How could you look them in the eye when they come home and find you've sold their pride and joy?"

Moose waved the card at her. "For Christ's sake, they were the ones who *wanted* to sell it first. The only reason they didn't was they couldn't find a buyer. Is it our fault we're better salespeople?"

"What just happened fell into our laps. Besides, how could I even try to make a living now I've sold the salon."

"You heard him? He said we could all keep our jobs." Moose held out the card and stabbed at it with a meaty finger. "See. He's an entrepreneur from Melbourne. That suggests to me he's not only well cashed up, he has no fucking idea of the embarrassing situation Joffa and Awesome Sauce got us into."

"Will you ever let up?" Joffa said.

Katy put her hands on her hips. "I don't know about you, Moose, but I'm not working for someone by the name of Sin. People would think this place was the second coming of Tiger Kowalski's Dancing School."

Moose scratched his beard as he thought back dreamily. "Whatever happened to that place?"

Katy tried not to gag as they crunched back across the gravel car park. "If you spent more time talking to people you'd know it was now a supermarket."

Moose held the door open for her. "Being a supermarket might be another front?"

Joffa fell in behind her, then came Moose. Tim was behind the reception desk with a big smile on his face, which told Katy he had recovered his equilibrium.

"We just got another email from the old blokes. They say they're in Galway," the Texan said.

"Jaysus," Joffa said. "What are they doing in Galway?"

"They've decided to spend the night there in a hotel."

"But why would they even go there? It's in the wrong direction."

Tim squinted at the screen. "They say the Grand Prix Simulator took them the wrong way."

"The what? Did they hire a Ferrari?"

Tim looked at the screen again. "No, a VW Golf, they say. Apparently it was a bit of a squeeze for the Mayor sitting in the back seat because he had to wedge himself in with one of the suitcases and all the overnight bags. But Wish-Wash — I assume it's him doing the writing — says serves him right because not only did he embarrass them on the plane, he was the S.O.G. who insisted hiring the G.P.S. instead of buying a paper map."

"S.O.G?" Moose's eyes narrowed.

"Silly Old Git," interpreted Katy. "But I have no idea though why Wish-Wash thinks G.P.S. stands for Grand Prix Simulator."

Moose laughed. "You know Wishy. He's never been shy of making shit up if he doesn't know the proper facts. Does the email explain how the Mayor embarrassed them on the plane?"

The young Texan shook his head. "That's perty-much it. Wish-Wash says they'll email again when they reach his castle."

"Typical," Moose said. "The old bugger can't help rubbing it in." He shook his head. *"His castle!"*

"Notice he doesn't say anyting about the weather," Joffa added. "It would be freezing over there this time of the year."

"I'd like to be a fly on the wall when they get an email from us that we've had an offer on the museum," Moose said. "You can tell them, Awesome Sauce, that we probably won't be here when they get back because we're retiring somewhere warm like Hawaii."

As soon as the computer keys started rattling, Katy rushed over to the counter. "Don't you dare send that, Tim!"

"Why not, Kazza?"

"We're not selling, especially not to him."

"Shouldn't we at least discuss it?" Moose searched Joffa's face for support. "Oh, I get it! We might be business partners but you two are always going to stick together."

Katy sighed. "We have differences of opinion all the time." She glanced at her husband. "Isn't that right, Joffa?"

He nodded.

"Let me guess? You usually give in to her for the sake of your sex life."

Katy sighed again. "You have a one-track mind, Moose. If you had ever got hooked up you'd know there is more to marriage than sex. But if you feel we need to discuss this offer, let's go upstairs now and talk it through before putting it to a vote."

She leant over the reception desk and retrieved a black and white leaflet she handed to Moose.

He looked down and saw pictures of washing detergent, fruit and pork chops in bubble-wrap. "What's this?"

"It's the weekly specials from Roses. You might find something to drool over at our meeting."

———

When Moose arrived in the lounge room, Katy and Joffa were already sitting on the sofa. So he sat down in the armchair opposite them, even though he knew it had dodgy springs.

"For someone so insistent on this meeting," Joffa said, "you don't mind keeping us waiting."

Moose returned fire with hostile eyes. "Not that it's any of your business, but I had to talk to Awesome Sauce privately if that's OK with you? It's not like it took an hour!"

"Will you stop bullying that kid," Katy said.

"I was doing nothing of the sort. I was just giving him some friendly advice, that's all."

"About what?" Joffa snarled.

"You tell me, know-all."

"Who are you calling a know-all?"

"Guys!" Katy said. "Can't we keep this meeting civil? We need to decide."

"You know my thoughts." Moose shifted uncomfortably in his chair. "Would it ease your conscience if we gave Oodles and Wish-Wash a share of the money?"

Katy tossed back her head. "I've already sold the salon! What are we going to do for a living?"

"Christ, I've already said," Moose said. "There's nothing to stop us from staying here and letting someone else worry about the bills."

Joffa raised his voice even more. "You still don't get it, do you? You don't think his name is a clue to how he makes money?"

"He can't help being born to that name. Sin might be a common name where he comes from?"

"You were out on you arse before Oodles and Wish-Wash brought you back into the fold," Joffa cried.

"You don't think I'm not torn?" Moose reached behind him and took a book off the shelf. "But we need to face facts. I've spent half my life looking for the Tasmanian Tiger for no return and this business if going down the gurgler. I say take the money."

He glanced down at the book in his hand and frowned. *"The Martian*! I never knew they made a book out of the movie?"

"You philistine!" Joffa said. "I think you'll find the book came first."

"Doesn't matter," Moose grumbled. "All books are born equal when it comes to ripping them in half."

"You really think you can?"

"I know I can. Watch!"

He gave it a good shot but couldn't, which just increased his feeling of frustration.

"So you're giving up?"

"We all have our off days."

"And yours are getting more frequent. You're obviously nearly ready for a dressing gown and a pair of fluffy slipp ..."

Joffa didn't finish the sentence because the flying book grazed his head, bounced off the back of the couch and landed on Katy's lap.

It hadn't even come to a halt when Joffa picked it up and hurled it straight back. It bounced off Moose's head and slammed into the bookshelf.

Both men jumped to their feet, and stood eye to eye. Moose could hear Joffa's racing breath.

"Any time?" Joffa said. "Old man."

"You make the first move because I promise you it'll be your last," Moose replied.

Katy was now on her feet, too, trying to prise them apart. "Fighting isn't going to get us anywhere." She pushed Joffa back into the red sofa, then shoved Moose back towards the blue chair. "You both should be ashamed of yourselves." She inhaled sharply and exhaled just as loudly. "If you two know what's good for you, you'll stay put while I go downstairs."

She closed the door behind her, but made a clip-clopping noise as she walked down the polished timber floor of the hall.

After her footsteps disappeared down the stairs, Moose said, "What's your missus up to now?"

"You know as much as I know."

"You reckon? I'd say I know a whole lot more than a muppet like you. Except for the Seven Dwarfs, of course. That would be your special subject on mastermind, wouldn't it?"

"I forgot you have some kind of degree in brickie's labouring, which officially makes you thick as a fecking brick."

"Yeah? Lucky for you I also did a first-aid course in Risdon, which means I'll know exactly what to do when I spread that nose of yours across your face."

"They let you participate in a first-aid course? What did you have to do? Play dead? They were short of CPR dummies, right?"

"Who are you calling a dummy?" Moose beat his own chest again. "I was undefeated chess champion for three years in a row in Risdon."

Joffa squinted and lowered his voice. "How come this is the first I'm hearing about this?"

"Not all of us are loudmouth skites."

"Who are you calling a loudmouth?"

"What are you going to do about it? Tell on me to your missus?"

"I don't have to. As it happens I was the chess champion at my prison, too, and I'll back myself against you any day."

"You're on. I've even got a chess set around here."

"Any time!"

"Bring it on." The problem was Moose couldn't remember where he had stored the chess set. In a box in the shed? Perhaps it was in a high cupboard?

He opened his mouth to speak but was interrupted by Katy coming through the door. She was holding a small leather case and closed the door behind her. "I could hear you guys arguing when I walked up the corridor! Do you want me to cut your beards or not?"

Moose and Joffa looked at each other.

Their beards were about the same length, but Joffa's was reddish-brown and Moose's was now more silver than the red it used to be.

Moose stood up, and stooped down to pick the book up from the floor. He slotted it back into a gap on the shelf. "I thought you had retired, Kazza?" he said softly.

"Yes, well, dad would probably roll in his grave if I ever let his sideline fall into the hands of the Northans." Katy unzipped the bag and pulled out a shaving brush, a cut-throat razor, a comb, and a pair of scissors, which she put on the kitchen bench. She tapped on the stool nearest to her. "So who's first?"

They eyed each other like two gunslingers waiting for the other to make the first move.

"For goodness sake," Katy said. "I'll decide then." She tapped the stool again. "Joffa, sit here. Moose, you can make yourself useful by fetching a towel."

When he returned from the linen cupboard in the hall, Joffa was seated on the stool and Katy was lathering up the brush in the sink.

He handed her the towel, which she draped around Joffa's shoulders.

"Now I get it," he said. "You never really planned to retire completely. The question is why you didn't tell Joffa and me earlier." He blinked slowly. "Or did you tell *him* and not *me*?"

"It was news to me, too," the Irishman said.

"He's not lying," Katy said. "The only person I told was Tim. You two have battered his self-esteem. I thought he needed a pick-me-up."

Moose slammed a fist into his palm. "I knew it! I wondered why Awesome Sauce was letting that fuzz grow on his face." He lowered his voice. "I guess this means he'll be coming upstairs too for his beard trim?"

Katy shook her head. "Someone's got to look after our six customers downstairs."

Moose's eyes widened. "How do you know we have six more customers?"

"Easy," Katy said. "They arrived when I was downstairs getting my bag."

———

When they filed down the stairs, Tim's face progressively crumpled when he looked from Moose to Joffa clean-shaven faces and then to the plastic bags Katy was carrying. "I thought you said I was next in line?"

"Nearly ready, I said. But not quite." Katy saw through the window the only vehicles in the car park were utes. "Have they gone already?"

Tim nodded. "They were in and out in 15 minutes, didn't even want tea or coffee."

"Did they say why?"

"One guy complained we didn't have the star exhibit any more."

"Maybe we should crank Gough back up?" Joffa rubbed a hand over his clean-shaven face.

For a brief time, Gough had produced a regular supply of bogus Tasmanian Tiger scats that had brought customers from far and wide until the deceit was exposed.

Tim broke back into a gawky smile, and he handed Katy a business card.

"What's this?" Katy examined it.

"One of the latest guests left it." He pointed to the writing on the card that said Trevor Wong was a software developer. "Looks like we're riding a gravy train with biscuit wheels. He *also* wants to buy the museum."

———

Katy examined her colleagues' puzzled faces. "Why do you think we've had this sudden surge of interest?"

Moose puffed out his chest. "They must have heard I'm about to be back on the job."

"As if!" Joffa made the universal hand signal for *you're a wanker*.

"Didn't I warn you guys?" Katy gave them another stern look. "I think something's going on that we don't know about."

"Like what?" Moose said.

"No idea. I have to take these bags of whiskers over to Gus. He keeps his ear to the ground so maybe he'll have some idea."

Joffa rolled his eyes. "That man names one cow correctly and people forever more think he's some kindle of oracle."

Gus had won the local newspaper's win-a-cow competition in 1994, back when he was still a biker who called himself Foetus. He sold the cow for a stake in a dotcom company, and made a huge profit when he sold the shares just before the bubble burst. Now he was a wealthy investment adviser and the best bush lawyer in town.

"The man's a legend," Moose said.

"I don't understand all the hero worshipping," Joffa said. "No one has told me about anyting he's done this century that puts him above us mere mortals."

"What are you talking about?" Moose threw his hands to his hips. "Didn't he give you the idea that launched this museum into the stratosphere?"

"As far as I'm concerned it was Oodles and Wish-Wash who made that happen. Gus might have planted some obscure seed in their heads but they're the ones I'll always thank for finding a dog to lay the golden scats."

"I'd love to stay chatting," Katy said. "But I have to get these whiskers to Gus while they're still fresh. Promise me they'll be no fighting while I'm out."

When she was on the other side of the door, Tim said, "What makes her think I'd be up for a fight?"

Then he whispered to Moose. "I did what you told me to do, by the way. I sent Oodles and Wish-Wash that email."

———

The light reflected on Gus's shiny forehead as he peered into one of the plastic bags. "This is a nice surprise. I was worried my supply would dry up with you having left the salon."

Gus and Katy were sitting either side of the desk in his office. He was squeezed in so tight, a roll of his beer-gut and the fat end of his unfashionably wide tie adorned with coconut trees and hula girls flopped over the desk top. He compensated for the lack of hair at the front of his scalp by growing his hair long down the back and tying it into a ponytail.

"Moose was worried you won't like his whiskers now he's going salt and pepper," Katy said.

Gus looked up and stared into space over her shoulder. "I did tell him that, didn't I?" Then he plunged his hand into one of the bags and ran the whiskers through his fingers. "Oh excellent! Excellent! I have to admit I like the marketing idea you've come up with. *A fine blend of whiskers and eyebrow clippings from the more mature bushranger.*" He withdrew his hand, brushing some hair from his fingers back into the bag, and looked up in time to see Katy shrug.

"You didn't really think I'd leave you in the lurch?" she said.

Gus pushed his chair back a little. "I didn't know what to think. I was trying to work out how to broach the subject with the V twins. I wasn't sure though how their old lady would take to it."

"I'm happy to talk to Vicki and Velda if you'd rather go with them," Katy said. "It wouldn't be the first time someone in the Northan family has turned a blind eye to something dodgy when there's money to be made."

"No, I'd be happier if you continued. I go a long way back with your old man. Besides, Joffa might have overtaken Moose in the quality of his clip, but Moose was the original bushranger and if this new line takes off in the U.S of A, he might have years left in him yet."

"If you put it like that …" Katy sensed the moment had arrived to hit Gus up for some free advice. "But there's something you can help me with."

"Sock it to me."

"It's really odd. When Oodles and Wish-Wash tried to sell the museum, they couldn't get a single bite. Yet we've had two separate offers in one morning."

"That's a good thing, isn't it?"

"It would be if we wanted to sell."

"But you don't?"

"It doesn't seem right. Last thing Oodles and Wish-Wash would expect is to come back from their holiday and find out we've sold the business to Mr Sin."

"To who?" Gus gasped.

"Mr Sin."

"That's who I thought you said. He never gives up, does he?"

"You know him?"

"He wanted to buy this business only weeks ago."

"What did you tell him?"

"Same as I told that other joker."

Katy put her hand to her mouth. "Don't tell me Mr Wong was the other guy?"

Gus nodded. "I never expected to cross paths with him again but I told him he could fuck off, too. Excuse the language."

"What's going on, Gus?"

The financial adviser shrugged. "I told them both if they didn't get out of town, I had some old friends just itching for a war."

"And that worked?"

"Eventually it did. Sin's first action was to try some high-pressure tactics on me. An hour after leaving this office, he had the audacity to ring and say he had another offer on the table, giving me only one hour to make up my mind. I told him not to waste time bullshitting a bullshitter, and repeated *my* ultimatum. When it comes down to it, blokes like them only understand one thing. *My men are better tooled up than your men.*"

The dragging feeling in her stomach had returned.

"You want me to call my boys in?"

"Noooo. Maybe both men have gone legit?"

"You reckon? My experience is bad guys only discover God and righteousness when they are on the brink of going to jail."

"Why did they want to buy into this place?" Katy waved her hand around the room.

"They didn't say, but I've got some ideas. It's got out I send shipments to the States."

"Is it that lucrative?"

"Not really. It's only one of the strings to my bow, but they obviously didn't know that. What I want to know is why they're back?"

Katy held out her palms and shrugged. "All I know is what I know. I've got two business cards of interested buyers."

Gus banged the table. "Just say the word and I'll fill this town with bikers."

Katy gave a nervous laugh. "Luckily the Mayor isn't around to see them."

Gus leant back in his chair and laughed. "I thought you'd be too young to even know about those good old days."

"Dad always talked about it." She sighed. "I'm pretty sure he wouldn't be laughing now though. If I know him, Dad's probably looking down, shaking his head over some of the stupid decisions I've made and turning heaven blue with his bad language. They'll probably turf him out of the place."

"They better not," Gus looked up to the ceiling, "IF THEY KNOW WHAT'S GOOD FOR THEM. My biker associates don't care where they have to go for some biffo." He banged the table again, then noticed the look on her face. "Something else worrying you?"

"Oh Gus, I think I've made a big mistake taking on the museum."

"Why do you say that?"

"Do you know how many customers we've had today. The place has been on a slow decline since we had to retire the dog. No wonder Oodles and Wish-Wash couldn't sell it?"

"But you just told me you didn't want to sell it."

"How can we? Those old men would never forgive us."

"But they'd understand if you're struggling to make ends meet."

"You were the one who told Sin and Wong to get out of town. Do you now think I ought to sell to one of them?"

"No, but if you've got two buyers knocking on your door, any real estate agent worth their salt will find more. How do you think they ramp up the price? Competition. Supply and demand. Dog eat dog."

"Moose is lobbying to sell to whoever comes up with the money first," Katy said.

Gus looked at her hard. "I would have thought Moose would know better than to tangle with those blokes. He's seen enough reptiles."

"Joffa and I really don't want to sell."

"Fair enough. But in that case you're going to have to do what Joffa did. You need to differentiate yourself from the other Tasmanian Tiger museums in the state." He scratched his balding forehead. "The problem you'll run up against is there used to be a lot of them to compare yourself with." His palm hovered just above the desk."Now? Not so many."

Katy threw her head into her hands. Joffa was right. Gus didn't really come up with ideas. He just waited for someone else to have a brainwave, and then he took the credit for it. Katy did have one idea but it was hardly earth-shattering and nothing she felt obliged to share.

But it was worth a try. She had some time to kill before her doctor's appointment.

———

The tiny woman who opened the front door had hair that had gone beyond grey, beyond silver.

Katy looked down on her snowy white hair, which seemed weird when she realised the old woman was standing one step up.

"You don't know me," Katy said loudly. "I'm Katy O'Fury."

"Have you found him?" The old lady looked up at her with sad eyes and her voice was strangled. Before Katy had the chance to answer, Mrs le Blanc said, "You'd better come in out of the heat, dear."

Katy followed the back of the pink floral dress slowly, patiently down the hall and into the kitchen where Mrs le Blanc beckoned her to take a chair at the table. With trembling hands, she filled the kettle at the sink, turned it on, then sat down opposite.

"I'm not from the police, Mrs le Blanc."

This produced sudden anxiety on the old woman's face, but Katy held up her outstretched palms. "I heard how someone's kidnapped your garden ornament though."

"You can call me Deidre, dear. Now we're down to six dwarfs and one dog."

"A dog?"

"You look as puzzled as we were, dear, when that thing arrived here on the back of a truck. Chalky told the driver he must have the wrong address but he checked his paperwork and said, no, this was the right place."

"Is Chalky your husband?" Katy asked.

Mrs le Blanc nodded. "A note attached to the ornament said it was a house-warming gift from our son. It was in his own handwriting, too, which came as a great surprise I can tell you." Her lips quivered. "But what could we do? The driver used a forklift to get it off the truck and position it in the garden. It was too heavy for us to get rid of, so we had no choice but to give it a name. Dog."

Katy smiled politely as the penny dropped. "Has this dog of yours got stripes?"

The old woman's wrinkles shifted on her face as she gave a crinkled smile. "How did you know that?"

"I think it's why I'm here. You obviously didn't know it's actually a statue of a Thylacine?"

"A what?"

"A Tasmanian Tiger."

"Really?" Mrs le Blanc turned her attention to the kettle, which was boiling now.

Katy watched the old lady warm the porcelain teapot with boiling water. She spooned loose tea into the pot, filled it with hot water and covered it with a golden-yellow woollen tea cozy. It was stinking hot outside but no way was a cold draft going to get between her and a hot cuppa. Next came the fine china cups from a cupboard and a plate of chocolate cream biscuits she laid out on the table.

"I'm from the Windy Mountain Tasmanian Tiger museum, Deidre." Katy said. "I haven't actually seen the statue. But Moose Routley has, and he'd know. He started hunting for the Tasmanian Tiger close to thirty years ago."

"Moose? Where have I heard that name?" Mrs le Blanc doubled the wrinkles on her forehead as she sat back down.

She pushed the plate of biscuits Katy's way.

"Oh, not for me." Katy actually craved tea but she really couldn't come at a biscuit. "But thanks, all the same."

"Watching your figure, are you? Just one won't hurt you, dear."

"I know, but really no."

"This Moose, he wasn't in the Armed Services?" Mrs le Blanc said. "They like their nicknames there. No one ever called my hubby Chalky before he joined the Navy. He was Cyril Le Blanc when he went in."

"I'm pretty sure Moose has never been in the Services," Katy said.

"I've heard that name somewhere. I must ask Chalky."

"Where is your husband?"

"He's out. Ever since that dwarf went missing he's been going out looking for him."

"He's driving around?"

"Oh, no. He's walking. He had to hand his licence in two or three years ago." Mrs le Blanc poured the tea.

"I was hoping to put a proposition to both of you."

"A proposition?" Mrs le Blanc poured the tea through a strainer.

"I was hoping you'd let us put Dog on display in our museum."

Mrs le Blanc's eyes sparkled as she handed Katy the cup with painted flowers and a gold rim on an equally pretty saucer. "That's very kind of you, dear."

"We'd replace him, of course. We'd get you a proper dwarf." Katy blew on the tea, then sipped it.

"I didn't know you could still get them?"

"Don't you worry. I'm sure between them, Moose and Joffa can make you one."

"Joffa?"

"Joffa's my husband."

"He knows how to make garden dwarfs?"

"They'd work it out between them."

"And they'd paint him the right colours?"

"Of course."

"And he'd be the same height as our other dwarfs? Because that's another of the things I don't like about Dog. He makes the dwarfs look small."

Katy looked at her watch, and realised she didn't have as much time as she thought.

"I hope you don't think I'm rude, Deidre, but I'll have to leave this tea. I'm due at Doc Jenkins's rooms in ten minutes."

————

After her visit to Doc Jenkins, Katy's head was in a whirl as she approached the museum.

Tim looked up when she came through the door. "Mr Sin called. He's given us an ultimatum."

Katy stopped and put her hands on her hips. "Did he just!"

"He gave us an hour to agree to the sale or else he says he's going to close another deal."

"What deal?" Katy continued to the front of the counter, and plonked her large handbag down.

"He didn't say. He was quite polite initially. He said he just wanted to know if you had progressed on your thoughts about selling the museum to him."

"And?"

"I told him another buyer had shown interest."

Katy smiled. "What did he say to that?"

"He sounded dark as a pocket. He wanted to know who the other bidder was but I told him I wasn't at liberty to say. And that's when he delivered the ultimatum."

"When was this?"

Tim turned around and looked at the clock on the wall. "Oh dang! Looks like the deadline has already passed."

"Doesn't matter," Katy said. "We're not selling to either of them. Gus reckons the same two guys tried to muscle in on his business a few weeks ago."

"You think they're up to no good."

"Isn't it obvious?" She picked up her bag and headed towards the counter gate.

Katy closed the gate behind her and put her handbag away. "Did the third bus arrive when I was out?"

"Sure did. It was only a mini-bus. But there were eight customers. That makes fifteen for the day."

"Where's Joffa? Out back with Moose?"

"I guess. It's awfully quiet out there."

———

Katy walked into the shed around the back, where Moose and Joffa were hunched over either side of a big wooden checkered-board.

"Shh," Joffa said as she approached.

She knew enough about chess to know the game was just beginning. Moose had the white pieces and had advanced a pawn. Katy watched Joffa move a black pawn. "You never told me you played chess?"

Joffa motioned for silence again, then addressed Moose. "It's your move, Boris."

Moose looked up darkly at him. "I can't believe you told your missus to shush up."

"You know what I think? You think if you can drive a wedge between us, it'll improve your chances of persuading one of us to side with you in selling the museum. Over my dead body!"

"Is that an invitation?" Moose said.

"Why don't you shut up and get on with the game?"

Moose did just that and moved his king bishop's pawn, and Joffa stared at him. "I thought you said you had been champion of Risdon?"

"I was. Everyone was scared of me."

"You don't think they were scared about what you might do to them if they didn't let you win."

"Are you going to play, or not?"

Joffa kept staring, then shook his head. "Didn't you ever learn about Fool's Mate? It takes a special kind of stupidity to lose in two moves." Joffa reached out and moved his queen, plonking her down and declaring, "Checkmate."

Moose stared at the position. "What the ... ?" He looked up at Joffa. "Bags we count this game just as a warm-up?"

Katy put her hands on her hips. "It's over? Joffa, I really need to talk to you."

"Go for your life." Joffa leant back in his chair and locked his hands behind his head.

She motioned to the door with a tilt of her head. "In private?"

"One of the joys of winning is sitting back and watching the loser put away the pieces while people in the public gallery also watch."

"But it's my chess set. You should at least help." Moose looked up to Katy for support.

Katy tapped on the side of the impressive chess board with its large carved Blackwood and pine pieces. "Where did this even come from?"

"It was kind of a farewell present after I left Risdon," Moose said.

"Don't they normally give you a farewell present *before* you leave?" Katy said.

"Are you kidding?" Moose ran a finger along the grain of the board. "All they let us have in there were plastic roll-up boards. My former cellmate had a friend send this to me after I got out. It's been gathering dust in a cupboard."

"Gathering dust just like you, I'd say," Joffa said.

Moose jumped to his feet, waving his fist.

"Oh, sit down, for goodness sake." Katy pointed to the chair, then looked down at her smug husband. "Joffa, I really do need to talk to you alone."

He shook his head. "Loser always leaves the ring first." He pointed a trembling finger. "Make him go and we'll be alone."

"You tell Joffa this, Kazza: I'm not going anywhere!" Moose said. "If this was a boxing match they'd be carrying *him* out of the ring on a stretcher right now."

"What's got into you two guys?" Katy said, looking from red face to red face. "Good thing I've got just the project where you're going to have to work together."

———

"You want us to make *what*?" Moose screwed up his face.

"I want you to construct one of the seven dwarfs as a concrete garden ornament."

"Why?" Moose looked up at her like he might look at a crazy person.

"I'm getting sick of people coming out of the gallery and asking me if I knew we have an empty cabinet on display. '*What happened to the dog turd?*'"

"Don't you think people will wonder why one of the seven dwarfs is now on display in a Tasmanian Tiger museum!"

Katy crossed her arms. "I'm not that stupid. We're not going to put the dwarf you make on display. We're swapping him for Dog."

"Dog?"

"That's what the le Blancs call that statue of a Tasmanian Tiger in their garden. Deidre le Blanc has agreed to let us have it if we can make them a suitable replacement."

Moose picked up the white queen, which he tossed from hand to hand. "And you know this? How?"

"I had a cuppa with her this afternoon."

"Jesus, Kazza! Haven't we got enough problems of our own without meddling in other people's affairs?"

"As soon as I heard the le Blancs had a model of a Tasmanian Tiger, I knew we had to have it. We need to make the gallery look busy again."

"It's a fucking garden ornament!" Moose slammed the queen down on to the board. "People who come to this museum will laugh when they see it."

"Have you got a better idea?"

"I do, actually! Sooner I get out there, sooner we can catch one that's real, not made of fibreglass. See the flaw in your plan? I can't be in two places at once. If I'm here learning how to make concrete garden gnomes, I'm hardly likely to be snaring a Tasmanian Tiger. I don't even know why we have to have this conversation. You know I was all for selling to Sin. Or Wong. Christ, they can buy it in partnership if they like. But you two howled me down."

"Do you want to hear what your friend Gus says about Sin and Wong?" Katy said.

"Gus knows them?" Moose's voice dropped.

"He said they were both here not long ago trying to buy his business so they could get their hands on the bushranger whiskers sideline."

"No-ooo?"

"He even offered to call in his biker mates to help if they cause us any more grief."

Now Joffa's eyes widened. "He's that worried, eh?"

Katy shook her head. "He says guys like that never take no for an answer."

"He might be wrong," Moose said.

"What?" Joffa said. "You're the one who put Gus up on a pedestal; now you're saying he might be fallible!"

"So you're happy to go into concrete dwarf production?" Moose replied.

"I'm sure Tim will help you," Katy said. "The blueprint is bound to be on the internet."

"Oh, right, Awesome Sauce would know." Moose's face contorted again. "Even if he doesn't, he'd make something up."

"You have to admit he knows his way around the computer," Katy said. "C'mon, it'll be fun."

"Fun? I can't wait to tell the boys in Block C what I do for fun these days!" Moose looked at Joffa again, but the Irishman stood up, shaking his head. "Sooner we start…"

Moose stared at the board. "What about my rematch?"

"It doesn't work like that. I'm the champion. You and Tim will have to play an elimination match for the right to challenge me."

———

Tim was sitting behind the desk at the computer when they came in.

"What do you know about building garden ornaments?" Joffa asked.

"And chess?" Moose said hurriedly. "What's that like?"

Tim rotated his hand. "Garden ornaments? Not so much. But you're in luck with chess. I was captain of my school team. Why?"

Moose closed his eyes slowly. "Shame there are still shards on the bedroom floor. Looks like you haven't got time for playing chess anyway."

Joffa turned to Moose. "You're always telling me how you used to be captain of the Windy Mountain Footy Team. Are you going to deny Tim his day in the sun? Captain v Captain, like."

Moose opened his eyes and held them open like he was daring Joffa to blink first. "When he finds all the bits of mirror, certainly. Because if I tread on just one shard, Awesome Sauce had better hide his nuts in a pouch before I give him a good kicking!"

Katy waved a finger at Moose. "Will you lay off Tim. You're going a funny way round if you even want him to find you a blueprint!"

"Who made you the boss, Kazza?"

She put her hands on her hips. "Someone has to act like the grown-up."

Moose pointed at Joffa. "If you're so grown up, can't you make this oversized brat give me a rematch?"

Joffa shook his head. "Who are you calling a brat? Rules are rules."

Moose balled his hands into fists. "Rules are like necks. They're made to be broken. Admit it: you're scared. When I shake off the cobwebs, you're going to wish you never tangled with me at chess."

"Is that so?" Joffa stood chest to chest. "You and whose army?"

Katy prised them apart. "I don't understand what's got into you guys?" She glanced at Tim. "The guys don't have time for fighting because they need to make a concrete model of one of the seven dwarfs."

"Which one?"

"It doesn't matter. Can you download some plans for a concrete dwarf with a beard and a little pointy hat?"

"Should be somethang on Youtube. How soon do you need it?"

Katy looked at the wall clock. "In the morning? It's been a long day."

She turned to Joffa. "We can have that chat on the walk home."

But Joffa shook his head. "I think I ought to sleep here tonight. It looks like we're dealing with bad, bad fellas here, and they might decide to try something." He eyeballed Moose. "I'm not putting my trust solely in *him*."

FOUR
HEARTBREAK HOTEL

MOOSE OPENED HIS EYES, and realised he could still hammering.

That was a relief. He had only been dreaming he was bunging a new head on the latest dwarf to come off the production line.

It took him a few seconds to realise there wasn't actually a production line, and he and Joffa were making a single garden ornament.

The noise was coming from downstairs. Someone was pounding on the front door.

It took even a few seconds more to remember Joffa was sleeping downstairs on the red vinyl sofa in the foyer. He couldn't possibly be sleeping through that racket, could he?

Knock-knock, knock-knock.

"For Christ's sake, I'm coming." Moose was buttoning his shirt as he stomped down the stairs. When he saw who was at the glass door, he regretted his choice of words.

Joffa looked up at him from his sleeping bag with the look of alarm. "It's Father O'Flaherty," he mouthed.

"No kidding?" Moose said. "What was wrong with you answering the door?"

"Keep your voice down, will you?" Joffa pointed across the room. "All my clothes are on the chair over there."

"All of them? You slept in the nude? In *my* sleeping bag!"

Moose was already at the door so he didn't have time to deliver further admonishment.

"Father," he said when he had opened the door. "I'm afraid Oodles has already gone to Ireland."

"I knew that," the priest said. "I was hoping you could get a message to him."

"Let me guess. You want him to kiss the Blarney Stone for you?"

Father O'Flaherty looked horrified. "I would never ask him to do such hocus-pocus."

"Good ting then," Joffa called out. "Blarney Castle is near Cork, down south. The old men are up north."

The priest craned his head, and saw the Irishman sitting up bare-chested in the sleeping bag. "Joffa?"

Father O'Flaherty was the one who had married Joffa and Katy, and Moose guessed he was probably wondering why O'Fury was there instead of the marital bed trying to bring more Catholics into the world.

"This is dedication for you," Moose said. "Joffa thinks being on *this* job early is more important than being on *that* job. So he decided to sleep over." He turned to Joffa. "Why don't you come over and shake Father O'Flaherty's hand?"

Joffa shook his head and his eyes looked frightened. He never slept nude when they were out camping. What made him think it was OK to do it now. How was he going to get out of this one?

Moose had his first big disappointment for the day when Father O'Flaherty said, "Oh, don't get up on my account, my son. I sleep in the nude myself." Then he addressed Moose. "Can you tell Oodles I'll no longer be able to perform private masses for him, or even public masses, for that matter. We've sold the church."

"Sold it!" Joffa hopped over in the sleeping bag and stood in front of Moose. His eyes widened as he clutched the top of the bag. "Can you do that?"

"The higher-ups in the church can. And they have. They need to raise money to pay for some unfortunate legal bills and settlements, and we weren't getting enough posteriors on pews it seems. So I'm being transferred to a more popular parish."

"Who bought it?" Joffa asked.

"Funny you should ask. Nice chap, despite his name."

Joffa's face dropped. "You sold it to Mr Sin, didn't you?"

"You know him? He says he's got big plans to convert the church into a cottage as soon as we can deconsecrate it. He says he doesn't even mind having a cemetery in his backyard."

"Why would he?" Joffa said. "It'd give him more options to hide evidence."

"What are you saying? He's up to no good?"

"You know he tried to buy this place first but we rebuffed him?"

"Maybe he really likes the neighbourhood?"

Joffa scratched his stubble. "It's more likely he's trying to muscle in on a little sideline we've got going."

The priest rubbed his clean-shaven cheek and lowered his voice. "You don't mean the Bushranger Whiskers black market business, my son?"

"Not you, too?"

The priest looked offended. "Of course not. I've shaved every day since I turned 17. The Bushranger Whiskers business is not much of a secret around here, among our brethren anyway."

Moose puffed up his chest. "The Mayor never knew about it; nor did the police."

"They're all Prodies. But I'm not even sure you're right about that. You don't just think they turned a blind eye?"

"Possibly. But that doesn't explain how a crime boss from Melbourne got wind of it."

"Crime boss? Mr Sin? He seems like such a nice man."

———————

As soon as Katy entered the foyer just before 8am she knew something was wrong.

The room was silent. Tim's head was bowed behind the computer and the two big men were sitting in the foyer with the kind of grim expressions she had only ever seen in dentists' waiting rooms.

"Is something the matter?" She came to a halt midway across the room. "It's not Oodles, is it?"

"He looked fine in the picture," Joffa said.

"What picture?"

"The one they attached to their email overnight. They've arrived in Donegal safe and sound."

"So why all the long faces?"

"You tell her," Moose said.

Joffa sighed. "Someone's bought the Catholic church."

Katy walked to the counter. "So?"

"It's who's bought it that's the problem," Joffa said. "Sin."

"*Our* Mr Sin?" she gasped, and nearly knocked her handbag off the counter. "Gus was right. Wong and Sin really think we are making big money from our sideline. He said they wouldn't take no for an answer."

"Perhaps Gus *is* making a fortune?" Joffa said.

But Moose shook his head. "I was the bloke who set this caper up in the first place, remember? It's no more than a small income stream for Gus, and he pays us handsomely despite that."

Joffa rubbed the back of his neck. "Looks like you're stuck with me here, Moose, until the dust settles on this. Can't see either of us leaving this building for any great length of time now."

Their heads turned when a mini-bus pulled up in a screech of brakes and flying gravel outside.

Rod Whish-Willson got out of the driver's seat and came to the other side to slide open the passenger door.

Out stepped three men, who were so heavily bearded they looked like undiscovered members of ZZ Top.

————

They disappeared into the gallery, and Katy fetched the barber's kit she kept in her cavernous handbag. "Do you have any more of those towels, Moose?"

He stayed unmoved in his chair. "Why?"

"It'll save you sweeping up hair from the foyer?"

Moose and Joffa looked at each other.

"Hurry! We don't know how long he'll be in there."

"Who?" Joffa said.

"The guy with the long beard."

"They all have long beards."

"His is the longest. When he comes out of the gallery, I'm going to tell him he's won a free haircut and beard trim, and his whiskers are heading for fame in the US."

Moose growled. "Are you kidding, Kazza? This caper has only worked for one reason: Nobody knows about it except us."

"That's not quite true," Joffa said. "You heard what Father O'Fla-herty said? Everyone in town knows about it."

Moose glared at him then turned his head back to Katy. "This will send a message to Wong and Sin they're on the right track?"

"Oh, I'm counting of that happening," Katy dragged a table to the centre of the room and set out her combs, scissors and a cut-throat razor. "In fact, as soon as you are done making the garden gnome, I think you two should change the wording of the sign out the front of the building. What do you think of *Windy Mountain Tasmanian Tiger and Bushranger Whiskers Museum*?"

She surveyed the makeshift barber shop. "Are you going to fetch those towels or not, Moose? I'm not the one who does the cleaning around here, so you please yourself."

Moose was shaking his head as he headed for the stairs. He returned a couple of minutes later with four large towels, and Katy took them from him and laid them out on the floor. Then she got Joffa to drag a chair over them.

"I really think you should rethink this." Moose was still shaking his head. "Nothing good can come of it."

Katy flicked her ponytail. "I don't know about you, but I'm not going to let those gangsters ride roughshod over me. I want to make this a regular thing. I want to shout it from the rooftops. I want to get as many people involved as possible. One lucky visitor a day wins a free haircut and beard trim. It needs to be in full view so everyone can spread the word. Imagine the publicity we'd get if someone takes a photo and it goes viral on social media."

"Good point," Tim said.

Both Moose and Joffa glared at him.

"Maybe," Moose said. "But that bloke looks like he's been growing that beard for a long time. What if he says he doesn't want it shaved off?"

"I think a mere trim off his beard will still give us plenty of whiskers."

It turned out though, Bob Johnson actually proposed she remove all of his whiskers.

He told Katy he had been growing his beard since he was 18. He was 34 now and it had grown down well below his chest.

As she wrapped the cape around him, he said he'd let her in on a little secret. "My wife told me not to come back from this end-of-season trip still with my beard."

"End-of-season trip? You look like musicians."

"No, we're the backline of the Dandenong Drovers Football Team. We used to be the forward line years ago but we kept being pushed back until now there's nowhere to go but hang up our boots."

Rod Whish-Willson looked at his watch. "This is going to put me behind schedule. What am I going to say?"

Katy ignored him. "Where's the rest of your team, Bob?"

"Bali." Bob held up a hand mirror to inspect his face. "Where did all those chins come from?" He sighed. "We're the three oldest members of the team and we've all done the bright lights. The three of us retired after our last game and we decided a cultural tour of Tassie was more to our liking."

"Why didn't you bring your wives?"

"Are you kidding? Karen has always looked forward to my end-of-season trips. She reckons it's a holiday for her, too."

He looked around at his two companions and they nodded in solidarity.

"I promised Karen that when I finally finished playing football, I'd shave off my beard. But have you seen the prices they charge in the shops? I was resigned to doing it myself."

Katy tilted Bob's head back the way she needed it and looked around the room. Bob's companions looked a tad envious, Rod was still looking at his watch, Tim was busy behind the computer, and Moose and Joffa's eyes were darting around the windows and doors like they expected Sin's and Wong's henchmen to storm the foyer any second.

"You need to relax," Katy told her partners.

"Easy for you to say," Moose said. "At least you're armed. Joffa and I haven't even got sharp scissors in our hands."

"Whoa." Bob's head jerked. "Who are you expecting?"

"You don't want to know," Joffa said.

Katy tilted Bob's head the right way again. "Don't you listen to them, Bob. Moose and Joffa worry too much." She looked over to them. "Haven't you two got work to do?"

When they had disappeared out the front door, Katy went to the bathroom and re-emerged with a bucket of hot water. She began lathering Bob's face.

Tim looked impressed when he saw the glint of the razor gliding over Bob's face.

"My turn next?"

"Not today, Tim." Katy tried to look impressed at the growth on his face. "A few more days should do it."

————

Moose peered over Joffa's shoulder. "Do you know what you're doing?"

Joffa was straining his eyes to study the blueprint Tim had downloaded.

The shed was illuminated by a single light-bulb that hung on a cord from the ceiling.

"Feck this!" Joffa waved the document. "This says we have to make a mould first."

"Can't we just buy one?" Moose said. "Even better, what's to stop us from buying the whole fucking thing?"

Joffa shrugged. "Weight, I suppose. It's got to be expensive to post a concrete garden gnome."

"Say we buy the mould? What then?"

Joffa studied the notes again. "Can you get your hands on a cement mixer?"

"I guess." Moose thought about his connections in the brick-laying industry. "I could make some phone-calls, call in a favour."

Joffa squinted at the piece of paper. "This says we also need a shovel, a jug, a rasp, a towel and …" His lips moved as he scanned the blueprint again. "… a vibrating table!"

"No big deal," Moose said. "I think I remember how to build one."

"That confirms you're a sicko if you know what a vibrating table is!"

"All a vibrating table does is remove the air bubbles in the concrete." Moose seized the opportunity to put in the boot. "You'd know that if the prison you went to had prepared you properly for outside life!" Then he thought it through further. "If you want my expert opinion though, I think we can skip it altogether. Those oldies probably have lousy eyesight, they'd never even notice a few bubbles."

Joffa looked around at him. "We don't want to fob them off with a faulty product."

"How do we know the model of the Tassie Tiger we're getting isn't defective? It might be riddled with bubbles for all we know."

"Katy won't be happy with a shoddy job."

"Just who wears the trousers in your family? I would have thought all the time you had inside would have toughened you up."

"Why don't you shut your gob before I do it for you?"

Moose felt the muscles in his face tightening. He waved a finger. "I'll ignore that. This time. But can you just explain to me why you are siding with her? Selling the museum would solve all our problems. It's not too late. Sin has obviously moved on but we can still accept Wong's offer." Moose rustled the blueprint in Joffa's hands. "Unless you actually prefer doing this bullshit!"

"I trust Katy's judgement a lot more than I trust yours! If she thinks the path to recovery starts with small successes, I'm happy to go with that."

"She got that bit right." Moose reached down and gestured around his knee. "You can't get much smaller than a garden ornament that just happens to be a dwarf."

Moose shook his head and turned to go back inside. "C'mon. Let's see if Awesome Sauce can order us a mould and then download the specs so we can build ourselves a vibrating table."

"I thought you said you knew how to make one already?"

"You're the one worried I might get it wrong!"

———

Sergeant Stretch came bounding across the car park just after Tim collected the plans from the printer.

Joffa and Moose were drinking coffee with Katy on the far side of the foyer.

"What's he doing here again?" Moose lowered his cup from his lips as he watched the blur of blue come through the door.

Stretch headed straight for the counter and laid down a small gadget. He was puffing. "I need to swear you all to secrecy."

"Is that all?" Moose said. "Is that why you're not wearing rubber gloves? No cavity searches today?"

"Very bloody funny!" Stretch folded in arms. "Do you really think I enjoy having to rely on people like you with criminal records? I just don't have any choice."

Tim resumed his seat, and put the printed sheets down beside him. "Do you want me to leave the room, officer?"

"It depends, son." Stretch looked over at Joffa and Moose. "I can't see *them* being able to give me the technical help I need." He doffed his cap towards Katy. "No offence, little lady. I'm sure you'd help if you knew how this works."

Tim stared at the silver thing on the counter. "It's a *memory* stick!" he said slowly.

Stretch scratched his head. "Is that supposed to mean something to me?"

"It's not like putting socks on a rooster. You just stick it in your USB port and follow the prompts."

Stretch gave him a deadpan glare. "Are you trying to be rude?"

Katy stood up and approached the counter. "Your computer must have a USB port."

"Not necessarily," Tim said. "Please tell me, Officer Stretch, your computer came out this century."

"Of course it did," Stretch said. "It was a replacement for the one we got in 1999." He blew out some air, which seemed to prompt him to pull the packet of mints from his pocket and offer them around. Tim was the only one who said he'd try one.

"But the new computer is still in the box," Stretch said, after he squeezed a mint into Tim's hand. "HQ says they'll send a technician out to set it up, but it hasn't happened yet. So we've had to take the old

Remington out of the cupboard. The young blokes had never seen a typewriter before."

Tim started chewing, then pulled a face.

Stretch looked down at him. "You're supposed to suck extra-strong mints, son, until you're able to properly grow a beard, or you're at least a legal immigrant."

Tim leant out of the policeman's sight but the clanging noise was strong circumstantial evidence he had just spat the mint out into the rubbish bin next to him.

Stretch looked over the counter in horror. "If I had known you were going to waste it …"

"Sorry, Officer. But I would have been happy to swing by and help with the computer."

Stretch put on his stern face again. "Do you really think I want to arrest you, son? You're not authorised to touch police technology, even more so being a foreigner."

Moose had wandered over to the counter, too. "That wouldn't be all bad. If you threw Awesome Sauce into jail, I'd get my room back."

Tim looked at him. "Is that the thanks I get for finding the plans for a vibrating table? I had to go into the dark web to find that!"

Stretch frowned. "Is there something I should know?"

Moose sighed. "Awesome Sauce is just trying to pull my chain. A vibrating table isn't what you think it is."

Stretch spoke slowly. "What is it?"

"It's for removing bubbles in concrete."

Katy added quickly, "We're just making something for the museum, Sergeant — a new exhibit."

This explanation seemed to satisfy Stretch, who pointed to the memory stick on the counter. "So can you make this thing work for me, son?"

"Sure thang." Tim reached out for the memory stick but Stretch's hand snapped down on his.

"Not so quick. You'll all have to promise not to reveal official police business."

"What's on there?" Katy said.

Stretch shrugged. "That's what we need to find out. It came with the first correspondence we had with the kidnappers."

They all filed through the gate in the counter, and gathered around the computer.

Stretch made them each raise a hand and swear after him whatever they saw on the computer would remain in this room.

Tim seemed the only one happy about the ritual. "Does this mean I'm now a deputy?"

"Shut up and get on with it, Awesome Sauce," Moose said.

Tim looked at him sourly, then plugged in the memory stick.

The video showed a tiny, colourful figure with tape over his mouth.

This dwarf was thin with a long, white beard, a red coat and a bulbous pink nose.

"As you can see, the dwarf is safe," a man said in a disembowelled voice Katy thought sounded like someone talking through an empty toilet roll. "You have precisely one week to hand over the money, or else Drongo gets it. We will be in touch."

———

After Stretch left, Katy scratched her head. "What money is he talking about?"

Moose scowled. "Christ, Kazza, it's not even our problem."

"I didn't see any greats signs of wealth up at the le Blanc place."

"Did you check under their mattress? For fuck's sake, we have enough problems of our own without trying to solve something Stretch is paid to do."

"There's no harm in thinking, is there?"

"With you, yes," Moose said. "We're supposed to be trying to get this museum back on track, remember? Why are you losing sight of that?"

"You're really not helping on the harmony front, Moose."

"That's hardly my fault." Moose pointed to his ankle. "I've been

cooped up for weeks but now I'm finally fit again, I should be getting
out there and tracking Tasmanian Tigers; instead, you've got me
making a garden ornament. Shit!"

"You'll thank me when we get that statue here in the museum."

"You reckon!" Moose pointed towards the direction of Bing Bong
Mountain. "You're not seriously trying to tell me you'd prefer a fibreglass figure instead of the real thing."

"Of course not. But how about we take one step at a time so the
museum is still a going concern when Oodles and Wish-Wash come
back."

The tinkling of chimes above the door made them turn around to
see a beaming Artie Rogerson coming inside.

———

"I wanted you to be the first to know. I'm off to Hawaii." Artie
Rogerson rubbed his large hands together. "I've only sold the bloody
building site!"

Joffa looked hard at him. "I didn't even know it was on the market,
Rog?"

"It wasn't. But I've really fallen on my feet this time. When the pub
burned down, I thought my retirement fund had gone up in smoke,
too. So I was surprised as you when this rich bloke came to see me
this morning. Now it turns out I'll be even better off. Waikiki, here I
come!"

Katy put her hands on her hips. "What rich bloke?"

"Goes by the name of Wong."

"Trevor Wong? The so-called software developer? What do you
know about him?"

"I know he carries huge wads of cash," Rogerson said. "He says he
won't even have to go to the bank."

"He didn't tell you he tried to buy this place first."

"No." Rogerson looked puzzled now.

Joffa scowled. "So you're fine handing him the licence as the town's new publican? What if he doesn't pass the test for being of good character?"

"Oh, that won't be a problem." Rogerson shrugged. "He's actually planning to build some kind of factory on the site."

"What?" Moose scowled at him. "What are we going to tell Wish-Wash when he comes back? He invested a good part of his life in that place."

"Don't I know it," Rogerson said. "But I'm pretty sure he'd be happy for me. He's still got his memories — and his momento."

"What momento?" Moose asked.

"You didn't know? When the pub burned down, Wish-Wash asked if he could have a keepsake from the ruins. He wanted the dwarf statue that used to sit at the end of the server in the little back bar. Problem was though it was very badly cracked and blackened in the fire, so I offered him the mould I used to make him."

"The mould?" Moose exchanged glances with Joffa.

"Which dwarf was he?" Joffa asked.

Rogerson pondered this for a moment. "I can't rightly tell you. We used to call him Sozzled."

Moose turned to Katy. "So what do we think made Wong change his mind about buying this place?"

"That's easy." Katy blew upwards, causing her fringe to dance. "I rang him back and said the museum wasn't for sale, not at any price."

"You did what? Behind our back?"

"It was hardly behind your back, Moose," Katy said. "We talked about it upstairs, remember?"

"That's bullshit! We didn't even know about Wong at that stage."

"No, but we knew about Sin. Same difference."

Moose looked from Katy to Joffa. "I bet you told him? I was right. I'll never be an equal partner while you two share pillow-talk. Christ, Kazza. I never keep secrets from you two."

"That's not quite true." All eyes turned to the Texan twang on the other side of the counter.

Moose grunted. "This is not the time, Awesome Sauce?"

Katy fixed her torpedo eyes on Moose. "I beg to differ." Then she turned to Tim. "What do you know that I don't know?"

Moose raised his voice and waved a finger at Tim. "You know you'll need a new head if you go blabbing."

Katy persisted. "C'mon, out with it."

Tim pointed back at Moose. "I was only doing what he told me to do when I sent the email to the old blokes. Ask him?"

Moose raked his hair with a hand.

"What did you tell them, Moose?" Katy's voice went up an octave.

"Christ! Don't you think the old blokes had a right to know someone was trying to buy the museum?"

The blood drained from Katy's face. "You did what!"

Moose clenched a fist. "Someone's got to talk some sense. Anyway, it's all a moot point now we have new neighbours. I'd say Oodles and Wish-Wash have moved on already judging by their email with those village girls. It was their way of telling us selling the museum is fine with them."

Katy frowned. "What village girls?"

"The email we got from them this morning. Joffa told you. The attached photo showed Oodles and Wish-Wash nursing pints of Guinness and village girls on their laps."

Katy glanced at Joffa. "He didn't tell me that."

"It didn't seem like the time," the Irishman said.

"And the Mayor was in this photo, too?" Katy said.

"Well, yes and no," Moose said. "He was in the background nursing what looked like a lemonade, and with a look on his face that suggested that village might have run out of good-looking young sheilas."

Rogerson had stepped back from the group, knowing from his experience of pub brawls it was best not to be caught in the firing line.

"Um, I'd better be going," he said. "I need to pack."

They watched him leave the premises and weave his way through the vehicles in the car park.

Katy put her hand around Joffa's waist and turned him around so he was shielded from the others. "I really need to talk. In private."

"Just as soon as we track down that mould," Joffa said loudly.

"Does that mean you don't need me to order one for you now?" Tim said.

"Put it on hold for now." He turned to Moose. "Where do you think Wish-Wash has put it?"

"Beats me. I've never seen it upstairs. It must be in the shed somewhere."

"Try the cupboard under the bench," Tim said. "I made the mistake of opening one of the doors once."

———

Tim was right. That's exactly where they found the latex mould.

Turns out Wish-Wash had quite a collection of memorabilia from The Applecart. Among these were ashtrays, beer coasters, bar towels, bar signs and assorted glasses. Behind them, Moose found the concrete-encrusted mould.

He threw it on the bench. "This is cause for celebration."

"What did you have in mind? You do know the nearest pub is in Slutz Plains now?" Joffa said.

"I was thinking more along the lines of a chess rematch."

"I'm already the champion. You'll need to play Tim in an elimination match first."

"You sucker punched me."

"I beat you fair and square."

"Maybe. But it only means you're the *indoor* champion. Can you stand up to the elements *outdoors*?"

"I can beat you anywhere, anytime," Joffa said.

This is how they came to drag a table and two chairs outside the shed.

It was when he was trying to remember which way around the queen and king went, Moose realised how quiet it had become.

He cocked his ear. "What's happened to all the tradies? They were here this morning."

Moose straightened his pawns, then turned his knights around so their heads faced towards the centre of the board. Although the pieces were large, they looked tiny in his enormous hands.

"You know it's touch move, don't you? That means if you touch a piece you have to move it."

Moose frowned. "We haven't even started yet."

"Sure we have. And you touched your rook pawn first. That means you have to move it."

"Yeah? Make me!"

"I can see I might have to do that."

"You and who else? Kazza's not going to help you."

"Leave Katy out of this. We *always* played TOUCH move at our prison."

"We didn't in Risdon — our only rule was if you took your hand off a piece, that meant the move was completed. I'm too old to change now."

Joffa smiled. "I keep forgetting you're getting on. Need me to go get you a cushion, do you?"

Moose held his gaze, and reached out and plonked his king's pawn forward two squares.

"You're fecking kidding me."

"Do I look like I'm kidding you?"

"You're a cheater, that's what you are. You were obliged to move the rook pawn."

"You should have told me you played by that stupid rule *before* we started."

Joffa exhaled loudly. "I'll let you off just this once. But from now on if you touch a piece, you have to say *j'adoube* first — or you have to move it."

Moose looked blankly at him.

"*J'aboube* is French for *I touch*."

Moose laughed. "Do I have to speak Froggy before I scratch my old fella, too?"

"No, but if you do you're not allowed to move *any* of the pieces until you go wash your hands. That would be my rule if it were my chess set."

"But it's not really mine."

"I thought you said it was a farewell present?"

"I said it was *kind* of a farewell present from a cellmate. I was told someone would drop by to collect it but no bugger's come calling yet. So the set is as good as mine. "

Joffa picked up a knight and examined it. "What's he inside for? Drugs?"

"No, murder and armed robbery. He got away with $90,000 in a bank job in the 1990s. They never found the money but they did find one of the tellers dead."

"That's it then." Joffa waved the knight. "One of these pieces probably has a little map secreted inside that tells us where the loot is hidden."

"Don't you think I've thought of that? I reckon it's some kind of a decoy. He probably expected me to turn the chess set into the police, thinking it would somehow throw doubt on his guilt. Whitey was always looking for ways to create smokescreens to confuse people?"

Joffa looked at the knight in his hand. "You reckon this is a trojan horse then?"

"I haven't worked that one out but I can tell you this ..."

Joffa waited for the words, but when nothing came he said, "What?"

"You've touched that knight, which means you now have to move it."

Joffa's face contorted. "I gave *you* a second chance!"

"You're right. A true friend wouldn't even let you touch that piece, not when he knows where it might have been."

Joffa frowned at him.

"I had an itchy back last night, OK? Haven't you ever had an itch in a place you just can't reach? Turns out that knight ..." Moose pointed to the knight on the other side of the board. "... or maybe that one, is the perfect little backscratcher."

Joffa closed his eyes slowly. "You're telling me I have a 50 per cent chance I'm touching the knight you used to scratch your sweaty back."

"If you put it like that ... ? I'd prefer to look on the bright side. There's a 50 per cent chance you're *not* touching the other black knight. I like to spread the love. I used that one to scratch my itchy arse."

Joffa slammed the knight back on its square.

Without speaking, he moved his king's pawn forward.

But he never got equality and struggled for about 25 moves before knocking his king over in resignation. He might have struggled less if he had dared introduce his knights into play. Instead, they stayed planted on their home squares, preventing the king from castling and eliminating any possibility of Moose being caught in clever knight forks.

Moose stared at the board jubilantly. "I can't believe you fell for that old trick?"

Joffa rubbed the back of his neck. "You never used the knights to scratch yourself? You bastard. It was a filthy, rotten lie."

"Guilty, your honour," Moose said. "It was the king you just knocked over I used to scratch myself."

He let that comment sink in and the whiteness he saw on Joffa's face told him it was time to change the subject.

"So, what are we going to do about your missus?" Moose said.

"I reckon she'll be more disgusted than me when I tell her about your dirty tactics."

"Not that. Just when I get fit enough again to go bush, the neighbourhood gets feral. Bad enough you and I have to stick around to guard the museum, she's got us making garden ornaments and now..." Moose pointed to the outside wall. "... She's thumbing her nose at them by cutting whiskers in plain sight."

When they heard the front door close, they had a line of sight down the side of the house.

They caught a glimpse of Katy crossing the road.

———

Katy sensed she was being watched as she trudged up the hill.

The feeling was confirmed when she arrived at the le Blancs' house in Hill Street.

The porch had the lingering smell of pipe tobacco, which suggested to her this was where Chalky was banished to when he wanted to smoke. The empty rocking chair was still moving.

Chalky would have had a good view of her coming up the hill. She imagined him opening the front door and yelling, "I think this is her." Katy could imagine Deirdre hurriedly removing her apron to reveal her best dress, and snarling at Chalky to put that damn pipe away as she went up and down the hall with a can of air-freshener.

Katy rang the doorbell and waited to see if she was right.

When Deidre answered the door, she did indeed looked flustered.

As Katy followed her down the hall, past closed doors, the dominant smell came from mothballs but also pipe tobacco and deodoriser.

A wall of heat hit Katy as soon as they entered the kitchen.

She fanned herself with her hands.

It certainly hadn't been as hot in here the other day but one whiff of the cooking smells and the sight of the cast-iron AGA oven told her Deirdre had been baking.

The table was set with a plate of scones, tubs of strawberry jam and cream, all atop a pretty tablecloth upon which sat painted porcelain cups and saucers, gleaming silver spoons and a green woollen cosy covering a teapot with steam coming out the spout.

"Are you all right, dear?" Deidre said.

"I'm fine. I just wasn't expecting it to be so hot."

"I'll get my husband to open a window." Then she called out, "Chalky."

A short, stocky old man appeared from another doorway. He was wearing a tattered green shirt with red suspenders, and his nose looked like something remodelled with putty after being broken too many times. "You called?"

Deidre glared. "I thought you were getting changed?"

"Give me a chance, D." Then the laden table caught his attention. "I obviously haven't got time to change now."

Deidre turned to Katy. "You'll have to forgive my husband. He's never let grubby clothes stand in the way of his morning tea." Then she addressed Chalky. "Can you open the window for Katrina?"

"It's Katy." She extended a hand to the former sailor. "Nice to meet you, Mr le Blanc."

"Oh, call me Chalky," he said. "I saw you walking up the hill."

"Chalky!" Deidre said.

"Well, I did." He turned his head towards his wife.

"Just open that sticky window."

Despite being only about 5 foot 3 and somewhere near eighty years old, he did that with surprising ease. The window protested creakily.

Then he took up a slumping position against the counter and watched as Deirdre, who was now sitting down opposite Katy, poured tea through a strainer into the two dainty cups. The niceties vanished when it came to his stained mug. But he didn't seem to mind as she poured him the strongest of the brew, tea leaves and all.

He reached down for his mug, which he put on the counter behind him. Then he stooped down to get a scone, but Deirdre slapped his hand away.

"Where are your manners? Guests first." Deidre looked up and her eyes followed a fly buzzing across the room. "My godfather! Did you have to let that fly in, Chalky?"

Deidre softened her tone. "Katrina is from the police."

"Oh no. The museum, remember?" Katy looked up at Chalky. "I'm *helping* the police though. That's why I'm here."

This was a little white lie. Sergeant Stretch knew nothing about her visit. But this time she really was on a mission to see if she could help. What made the kidnappers think the le Blancs even had *the money*? Looking around the room, the embroidered tablecloth, the row of Toby jugs on a shelf and fancy glassware in a china cabinet might be the peak of their riches.

Chalky raised his mug to his lips.

"We should be able to get the new dwarf to you in a few days," Katy said. "Either Joffa or Moose will deliver it and they'll take away Dog."

Chalky blew on to his tea as if he was making space for him to think about this. "You'd better send both of them. Dog is heavier than he looks."

Chalky squinted at the Toby Jugs, though he didn't appear to be focused on them at all. "D told me about those two blokes. Moose? Moose? Where have I heard that name?"

Chalky locked eyes with his wife. "I don't know why we had to get the police involved?" He looked somewhere between sad and angry. "I knew that handwriting as soon as I looked at it. I just don't know how he did it? Or why?"

———

Moose opened the door for Katy.

"Where have you been?" he said, as she swept past him into the museum.

"I've been up at the le Blancs."

"Again?" Moose looked over to Joffa, who was minding the seat at the computer for Tim who had gone upstairs.

"Calm down," Katy said. "I just wanted to reassure them the dwarf garden ornament is nearly ready."

"You expect us to believe that? Why don't you let Stretch do the police work? It's probably only kids anyway."

"You think so? It's not what Chalky thinks."

"Who's Chalky?"

"Old man le Blanc."

Moose held up his palm. "I really don't care what he thinks. AND NEITHER SHOULD YOU."

"You're not worried that Stretch looked worried? And with good reason, as it turns out."

"For fuck's sake, Kazza, will you listen to me? I don't WANT TO KNOW."

Both Katy and Moose turned their heads when Joffa entered the conversation. "I have something here you *will* both be interested in." He pointed to the screen in front of him. "The old men have sent us another email. This time they want to know the best way to remove a snake from their kitchen."

Katy laughed. "This is payback surely?" She looked darkly at Moose.

Joffa was shaking his head. "Everyone knows St Patrick chased all the snakes out of Ireland."

Moose smirked. "Maybe the mixed-up Mick got mixed up and actually chased all the Native Cats out."

Joffa balled his fists as he stood. "I think the time has come to sort this out outside. And I'm not talking about playing chess this time."

"Joffa!" Katy said.

"You heard him!"

Moose threw his hands up. "Can't anyone around here take a joke?"

Katy turned her sights on him. "Have you told Oodles and Wish-Wash you were joking about selling the museum?"

"That wasn't a joke, and you well know that."

She thought for a moment. "I'd hoped you'd set them straight though now we've rejected both offers and they've invested elsewhere."

"Not my job." Moose squeezed his chin. "Anyway, we have no way of knowing if another prospective buyer will turn up?" He eyeballed Katy. "If we continue to make a public spectacle of the beard-cutting spectacle, we might attract a lot of fucking interest."

"At least I'm doing *something* to try to increase our income. What are you doing to save the museum?"

"Are you kidding me? You're the reason I'm not getting out there and tracking down a Tiger. I'm confined to barracks, making fucking garden gnomes and protecting you."

"Why do you feel the need to swear at me?" Katy pointed at the door. "Go, if that's what you want. I don't need your protection."

"Fine," said Moose. "I'll take Awesome Sauce with me. *Somebody's* got to teach him the difference between a Tasmanian Tiger and a Native Cat."

"You never let up, do you?" Katy said. "Don't expect much sympathy from me when you come limping home. It'll serve you right for trying to walk over rough terrain before you're ready."

"That's where you are wrong. My doctor has given me the all clear." Moose raised his leg and rotated it again.

"When did he give you this diagnosis, pray?"

"Christ, Kazza, do you think you're the only one who leaves this museum for secret rendezvous."

They all turned their heads when they heard footsteps.

The Texan was singing to himself as he came down the spiral stairs.

"I don't know why you're smiling, fuzzy features," Moose growled.

———

Katy and Joffa stood outside watching Moose and Tim trudge up the road with their heavy backpacks.

"Well, that's that," Katy said, as they disappeared up the High Street towards the trail to Bing Bong Mountain.

"So who does the old man think kidnapped the garden ornament?" Joffa said. "Wong or Sin?"

"Neither of them. He thinks their son is behind it."

"Their son? What the …?"

"That's what I thought. Things are starting to spin out of control around here. I wish Moose had stuck around."

Joffa looked at her. "It was you who told him to go."

"I didn't think he'd really do it."

"Judging by the size of those packs, Moose is taking enough provisions for a long stay out."

Joffa turned to go back inside.

Katy followed. "Why can't Moose see I've got the best interests of this museum at heart? And I really do hate seeing you and him at each other's throats."

"Look on the bright side." Joffa laughed. "He's really going to flip when he returns and finds out I've been sleeping nude in his bed."

"Joffa!"

Joffa lifted the gate on the counter. "Someone has to stay here now to guard the place, but you don't think I'm gonna keep sleeping downstairs in his sleeping bag."

Katy followed him and tried to push past him and beat him to the computer, but he put out his arm to stop her.

"I need to google someting?"

"I can do it for you."

"No, I can manage. We could do with some extra muscle around here while Moose isn't around. I want to know if Big Jake is free to help us."

Katy sighed. "By free you mean?"

"That's exactly what I mean. Big Jake used to be a cellmate of mine. He's not always available."

————

Katy cooked a steak for Joffa upstairs, in the hope that she'd now have the chance to share their news.

But she soon realised the seating arrangements weren't ideal. Instead of sitting opposite gazing into each other's eyes, they were now sitting side-by-side on stools staring at the wall.

Joffa sawed off a portion of meat and put it halfway to his mouth before stopping. "We're better off without Moose, anyway, especially if I can track down Big Jake."

"Joffa, can we talk?"

When he had swallowed, he turned and said, "We *are* talking!"

"But do we have to talk about this?"

"Are you kidding? I'm racking my brains trying to work out how I can track down Big Jake because I really think we need him here."

Katy looked blankly at him. "He sounds like another expense we can't afford."

Joffa touched her cheek. "Don't worry. Big Jake does a lot of pro bono cases."

"Oh, he's a lawyer. Why didn't you say?"

"Because he's not. He's a thug who only exacts payment if he wins — and only then by plundering from the loser."

FIVE
DON'T BE CRUEL

KATY WAS BACK behind the computer just before 8am when she heard creaking behind her. She turned around and saw Joffa was coming down the stairs on crutches.

When he reached the bottom, she saw his foot was wrapped in a towel fastened with string. "You're bleeding!" she shrieked.

"The red towel makes it look worse than it is."

"What happened?"

"I should have listened to Moose and not walked around in bare feet in the middle of the night." Joffa stretched his thumb and forefinger. "You should have seen the size of the shard of broken mirror I pulled out of my sole."

Katy lowered her voice. "You didn't get blood on Moose's sheets, did you?"

"Not a drop." Joffa paused. "I decided to sleep in Tim's bed. Serves him right if he finds a few drops of blood."

"So it didn't bleed much?"

"Are you kidding? When I pulled the shard out, it was like breaching a dam wall."

"But you said a *few* drops of blood?"

"That's right. That's all you can see from the top of the bed. I wasn't game to peel back the covers to inspect the damage down lower."

Katy rolled her eyes. "I'll have to go up and change the sheets."

"No need. I'm planning to transfer to Moose's bed tonight."

"Do you want me to make an appointment with Doc Jenkins?"

"What for? I didn't cut off my foot."

"No, but someone needs to clean and dress your wound. You say you pulled out the shard. But did you get all of it? I don't even know why you didn't go to the hospital last night."

Joffa looked at her darkly. "How was I supposed to get up to the hospital in the shape I was in?"

"You've got Moose's crutches."

"I found them *this morning*, not last night." He looked from side to side like he was inspecting a police line-up. "I love one of these crutches but I hate the other one. Problem is I don't know which one of them was used to smash the mirror."

"I'll ring Doc Jenkins's rooms."

"No need. I'm sure it'll heel itself."

"You don't know that."

Joffa screwed up his face. "You know I really don't like doctors." Joffa held Katy's stare. "You heard Moose, there should be a law against a doctor having a son who's an undertaker."

"Are you scared?" She used two fingers to vibrate her lips. "You're worried the nasty man might give you a big needle? Diddums!"

He shot a finger her way. "We have to think about the cost, too. How are we going to tighten our belts if we hand money over willy nilly to some quack?"

"Who told your Doc Jenkins was a quack?"

"I've heard Wish-Wash say many times dat's the case."

Katy gave a wry smile. "Oh, he'd know! Do you know how much alcohol that man consumed years ago, and the cold nights he had sleeping rough. When Doc Jenkins arrived in this town 20 years ago, he inherited Wish-Wash's healthcare. A lesser doctor might have referred him to specialists in the city. But Doc Jenkins kept seeing him.

If he is such a quack, how do you explain how Wish-Wash is even still with us?"

"Do you know how many trips I've had to the doctor in my 37 years? My ma didn't even invite a doctor to my birth. She had me at home, with just a midwife who got the shock of her life to deliver a 10 pound 2 ounce baby."

Katy's eyes widened. "How big?"

"All the men in our family start out big and just get bigger."

Katy picked up the phone.

"Who are you calling?" Joffa said.

"Who do you think? Hopefully, they can fit you in first thing. But when you come back we really do need to talk."

———

Joffa sat alone in the waiting room for at least 20 minutes, which was all the time he needed to read all the guff on the noticeboard but not enough time to make him feel he had to resort to one of the out-of-date magazines. The notices told him where to go for birthing classes, one poster implored him to stop smoking, particularly if he were an expectant mother, and another extolled the virtues of the local playgroup.

"Mr O'Fury?" the receptionist finally said. "You can wait in Room One. The doctor will be in presently."

Joffa swung in on his crutches, the towel tied to his bloody foot.

As soon as he sat down, he wished the receptionist had invited him to bring one of the magazines in from the waiting room. You could only look at the health charts on the wall for so long. How much more milk could one person drink, where did you even catch Omega-3 rich fish? The crayon drawings of colour-coded stick people were presumably from happy young patients, which made even more sense to him when he saw the jar of jellybeans on the desk. He was just about to help himself to one when the skeleton that stood at the foot of the bed along the side wall caught his eye. Joffa hopped over to inspect it more closely.

Just as he bent down, someone closed the door behind him and Joffa looked around to see a man in a white coat examining the file he carried. "How can I help you … Mr, um, O'Fury?"

So this was Doc Jenkins?

His appearance challenged the notion most sons ended up looking like their fathers.

Doc Jenkins was about 6 foot 2, with a pot belly and dark bags under his eyes, whereas Dave, the undertaker, was short, dumpy and bright-eyed. Dave was pushing forty, so his old man must be closing in on retirement. It was hard to tell. Sixties? He might even be pushing seventy.

"Everyone calls me Joffa." The Irishman stuck out his swaddled right foot. "I trod on some broken glass. I didn't want to worry you with it, but Katy insisted."

Doc Jenkins squinted. "Katy?"

"My wife, Katy McDonnell."

"Oh, that Katy. That would explain why you were doing a jig in bare feet then."

"What?"

"Didn't Katy tell you about her visit here yesterday?"

Joffa's eyes widened. "She didn't even tell me she was sick?"

"Oh! You don't know?" Doc Jenkins dropped his voice. "You'll have to ask her about it, my boy. I'm bound by doctor-patient confidentiality."

Doctor Jenkins motioned for Joffa to lie on the bed. His glasses were hanging on a chain around his neck, and he put them on. "Mind you don't kick George."

"George?" Joffa lifted his head from the pillow.

"My skeleton. It took me ages to put him back together last time."

The doctor pulled a chair over to sit on and unwrapped the towel. He examined the cut and shook his head. "You've done a good job of that. Stay here."

He left the room and returned with a tray, upon which was a bowl of liquid, a bottle, a small pair of scissors, tweezers, a scalpel and some other items, including a hypodermic needle, which he placed on a trolley he wheeled over.

Joffa pointed to the needle. "What's that for?"

Doc Jenkins sat down again and lifted Joffa's foot carefully. "I'm going to have to clean the wound so I can get a good look at it. I might need to prod around to make sure there are no fragments of broken glass inside. So you'll be needing a painkiller." He looked up at Joffa. "How did this happen?"

Joffa sighed. "I trod on some broken mirror."

Doc Jenkins shook his head.

"*I* didn't break it! Our resident ejjit thought the best way to remove it from the ceiling was to smash it to smithereens."

Doc Jenkins chuckled. "Oh *that* mirror. Billy Gumboots had that installed years ago."

"You know about that?"

"Everyone knew. George Pickles installed it for him, and George liked to brag. He used to spend a lot of time in The Wind Tunnel Cafe so he had a ready-made audience."

Joffa leant back on the pillow. "I wonder why I've never run into him?"

"How long have you lived here? Poor George died a few years ago. I wrote his death certificate."

Joffa lifted his head towards the skeleton. It couldn't be, could it?

The doctor picked up on his discomfort. "Don't worry. Different George." He looked lovingly at the skeleton. "We've been together for so long. I got him when I worked at the prison infirmary at Risdon, and that was a while ago."

He got up and fiddled with something on the trolley. When he turned around he was examining a loaded needle.

The needle wasn't pleasant but it was over in a jiffy.

"While that's doing its job, I'll go and see another patient in Room 2. Stay put, don't touch George, lie down and relax."

When he returned, the foot was numb and he went to work.

Joffa didn't dare look, but he could tell by the oohs and aahs and the clatter of the bowl and other instruments the doctor was going to work.

"The ting is," Joffa said, as he laid back on the pillow. "I wouldn't have even been sleeping in that room above the museum if we weren't worried about the new fellas who have moved into the town."

"What new fellas?"

"You haven't heard? A fellow by the name of Wong has bought the pub construction site, and a fellow by the name of Sin has bought the Catholic Church. We think they're both up to no good."

Joffa heard something drop to the floor.

———

Joffa was surprised when Sergeant Stretch opened the museum door from the inside.

"Why are you here?" Joffa asked, as he swung past the policeman.

"I could see you were having difficulty with your crutches weaving past all those cars."

"I don't mean why are you opening the door for me. I mean why are you here at the museum." Joffa swung over to the counter where Katy smiled up at him.

"We need to talk," he whispered.

Katy tilted her head, which made him spin around on his crutches, and he saw an elderly man and woman sitting in the foyer.

"We've received another communication from the kidnappers," Stretch said. "We've come by to use your computer." He waved another USB stick and gestured towards the old couple. "Have you've met Mr and Mrs le Blanc?"

Joffa nodded to them. "You'll have to excuse me for not coming over. Doc Jenkins says I've got to minimise the weight on my foot for a few days, and these crutches are murder on my armpits."

Joffa's right foot was swathed in clean, white bandages.

"Katy told me you trod on some glass." Stretch shuddered. "Ouch!"

Joffa looked at the USB in Stretch's hand. "I thought the kidnappers had set a week's deadline."

"That was my understanding, too." He put the USB down on the counter. "So I was very surprised when it turned up in our letter box this morning, accompanied by a note that said we had been warned it wasn't going to be pretty watching the video."

The sergeant pulled a roll of mints out of his pocket and walked across the foyer to offer them to the old folks. When they waved him away he walked back over and offered them to Joffa and Katy but they shook their heads, too. "Please yourself, all the more for me." He popped one into his mouth. "I suggested to Katy we wait until you were here, in case she needs your shoulder to bury her head in."

Stretch started his crunching. "I was hoping your young American guru would be here but the little lady says she knows how to operate it."

"Any further ideas about who might be doing this?" Joffa said. Stretch shook his head.

"He ought to know we haven't got any money." This came from the old man, who was now on his feet and heading towards the counter, his wife right behind him. "And we wouldn't give it to him if we did."

The surprise showed on Stretch's face. "I thought you said you didn't have a clue who was behind this?"

Chalky turned around sharply, as if he had been poked in the back of the ribs, then turned again almost as quickly. "Er, I meant the bloke on the video."

Stretch didn't push it. All he said was: "Chalky and Deirdre haven't seen the latest communication either, so we all need to brace ourselves."

They all converged behind the counter around the computer.

"Ready?" Katy said as she held the USB stick near the slot.

"You sure you know what you'd doing, little lady?" Stretch said. "We don't want Tim coming back to a broken computer."

Katy smiled at him. Joffa knew that was her restrained look.

Stretch directed his next comments to both Katy and Joffa. "Remember? What you see and hear here today is top secret."

Katy inserted the USB stick.

It took a few moments for the video to load and fade from black to a hooded figure holding what looked like a concrete cutter.

"Tricked you! Bet you didn't expect to see me so soon," came the toilet roll voice from behind the black hood. "But don't say we didn't warn you." He plugged in a water hose, hit a button and the chainsaw-like device roared into life.

The camera panned to a beige coloured bag, which was removed by a hand to reveal the kidnapped dwarf, still with the tape over his mouth,

"Drongo must now die because of you."

Chalky grimaced.

Everyone winced when the hand reappeared and ripped off the tape over the concrete dwarf's mouth.

With clouds of dust flying into the air as the teeth of the concrete cutter sliced noisily through the garden ornament's neck, his head finally tumbling to the ground.

The hooded man turned off the cutter and gave an evil laugh as he looked down at the severed head. "We'll be in touch." The video faded to black again.

The computer pinged, signifying the arrival of an email.

Stretch stared in amazement. "That was quick. How did they know we were even here right now?"

Joffa looked at the wall beyond which was the construction site. He had noticed when he had weaved through the car park the utes were different. Different makes, different colours, different number-plates. It appeared Artie Rogerson's entire workforce had been replaced by Wong's men who had probably come across on the ferry. Even if they were legitimate construction workers they'd have concrete cutters for sure. And they had a bird's-eye view of who came in and out of the museum.

Katy snapped him out of his musings.

"The email is actually from Donegal," she said.

"You sure? Not from those sicko's?" Stretch said. "If there's a case for bringing back the death penalty in Australia, we've just witnessed it."

Joffa looked at him blankly. "It was a *concrete* dwarf."

"Criminal behaviour progresses." Stretch slid his hand across his throat. "Dwarf today, who knows who gets it in the neck tomorrow?"

Joffa looked at his watch. "Jaysus, who'd be emailing us at two in the morning from Donegal?"

Katy adjusted her reading glasses and scanned through the email. "That would be Wish-Wash." She read some more, then said, "I'd better tell you later, Joffa."

————

Joffa and Katy stood at the window watching Stretch and the old couple disappear towards the town centre.

As they turned, he felt her brush the fingers he had wrapped around one of the crutches. "What did Doc Jenkins say about your foot?"

"I think it's outrageous he charges by the stitch?" he said. "I probably would only have needed one stitch but the quack widened the insertion point with a scalpel so he could dig out another glass fragment."

Katy smiled. "A lesser doctor might not have found it."

"I've only got his word to say there was even an extra piece in there," Joffa said as he came to a rolling halt in front of the counter. The problem was he had kept his eyes closed during the surgery, and the only actual evidence he saw was the itemised bill, which made his blood boil when he realised they charged extra for every stitch.

He sighed. "You never told me you needed to go to the doctor yesterday."

"That's why I needed to talk to you, Joffa."

"Whatever happens, don't let him give you stitches."

She suddenly looked pale.

"You all right?"

"I'm … fine. A bit of nausea. Nothing to worry about. I was just, um, thinking about that email from Donegal. Wish-Wash now says they've cornered a Tasmanian Tiger."

"He says what!" Joffa's voice rose sharply. "In Ireland? Jaysus, how does he think a Tasmanian Tiger got there? As a stowaway on a wing of their plane?"

Katy shrugged. "He says in the email the snake was all a misunderstanding, but that was all James Northan's fault. He says he, Wish-Wash, not the *dozy* Mayor, went downstairs for a glass of water in the middle of the night and found a Tasmanian Tiger rummaging through the bin in the cupboard under the kitchen sink. He says he's now locked it in the kitchen and is standing by for instructions."

Joffa didn't have time to answer because their heads turned when they heard gravel flying and the sound of brakes.

It looked like Wash-Wish was back with his mini-bus.

Nine people climbed down, including a young man with a backpack and a blond beard.

———

Joffa watched Katy go to work on the man's beard.

His whiskers were falling on to the drop-sheet in the foyer while the other guests were inside the gallery.

Their conversation was conducted in broken English interspersed with German words Katy had obviously learned at school, and Joffa didn't understand anything from their exchange. He wasn't sure the backpacker really knew what was happening either.

"Vhat ist bushranger?" he asked.

Rod was standing by watching. He was now wearing the company's uniform of sky-blue blazer and green shorts rather than the kaleidoscope of fashion crimes he had worn on his first day. He said to

Joffa, "I thought this bloke would fit the bill. That's why I picked him up."

"You mean he's not actually on the tour?"

"Not really. Don't tell anyone. I picked him up on the side of the highway. He was trying to hitch a lift to Hobart."

"Jaysus! You didn't tell him he was going the long way?"

"Are you kidding? Nice beard like that! I ought to be getting commission."

"You're right." Joffa bent down and picked up a clump of hair and held it up. "Here's your cut."

Katy stopped snipping. "Don't you listen to him, Rod. We'll have a nice little something for you later."

"Unless you'd actually prefer short and curlies in a brown paper bag," Joffa added.

Katy glared at her husband. "Haven't you got anything better to do rather than tease Rod?"

"What?" Joffa said. "I don't think I can proceed without Moose's expertise."

Joffa looked slowly around the room. "Speaking of expertise, did I tell you I worked briefly as a security guard? In my expert opinion, I'm not sure it's a very wise course of action to cut beards out in the open. What if they see from next door?"

Katy pointed to the brick wall with her scissors. "Hello? Visual barrier."

"You don't think they'll notice when a man carrying the same backpack he went in with when he was hairy leaves the building with a denuded face."

"I think they'll be too busy with their power tools to notice."

"That's another good point. Do you reckon they've got a concrete cutter over there?"

"You heard Chalky. He's convinced his son is behind the whole thing."

"When did he say that?"

"Didn't you hear him say *he* ought to know they didn't actually have any money?"

"Yes, but he clarified that. He said *he* was the man on the video."

"That was entirely for Stretch's benefit. I wouldn't be surprised if he hasn't got a bruise on his back in the shape of Deidre's fist."

"She hit him?"

"She made him reconsider his words in front of Stretch."

Joffa replayed it all in his head. "Now you mention it, that makes sense … but what if the old man is wrong? What if the reason Wong bought next door and Sin bought the church is they're BOTH involved in the kidnapping?"

Wash-Wish's eyes almost popped out on hearing all this. "The museum is in the middle of a kidnapping! Really?"

"Not a word to your grandfather, Rod," Katy said. "It's only a concrete dwarf but Wish-Wash has a penchant for getting melodramatic." She resumed her snip, snip, snipping and addressed Joffa again. "Gus reckons Sin and Wong are only trying to muscle in on the bushranger whiskers business."

Joffa repeated this in a sing-songy voice. "*Oh, Gus reckons they're still trying to muscle in on the bushranger whiskers business.* It must be right then. The man's a fecking genius. Moose says so, even Wish-Wash says so."

"How dare you ridicule my grandfather," Rod shouted.

"Ridicule him! The man must be back on the turps the way he's been trying to ridicule us. Poteen probably." He looked over to his wife. "Tell him Katy! Tell him what Wish-Wash told us in the email. Tell him what he reckons he saw in the kitchen of his *castle*?"

Katy nodded. "Wish-Wash is claiming he's cornered a Tasmanian Tiger over there, Rod."

"And you don't believe him?" Rod said.

"Jesus, Mary, and Joseph," Joffa said. "What in God's name would a Tasmanian Tiger be doing in Ireland? We can't even find one in Tasmania!"

"Maybe that's why? They've all emigrated. It's lucky my grandad is over there, I'd say. Who better to ID one than a *world expert*?"

Joffa sighed. "Wish-Wash's *alleged* sighting was at the height of his career as *town drunk* in 1967. Would you take the word of a town drunk when he claims he was woken up in the middle of the night by a wild animal last seen alive more than 30 years before?"

"He doesn't lie." Rod looked around to Katy for support. "Not about big things like that anyway."

When the front door opened, all eyes turned.

"Good day," said the short, stout man who entered. "Remember me?" Sin's eyes fell on the makeshift barber's chair. "Seems like I've come at the right time to become an actual bushranger."

———

"You're mistaken, fella," Joffa snarled.

Kate waved her scissors, as if she was calling off a Rottweiler. There was no point denying what she was doing. Blind Freddy could see the backpacker's whiskers were scattered over the drop-sheet on the floor. "This is a one-off shave," she told Sin. "If you go up to the salon in the town centre, I'm sure Vicki or Velda will be able to help you."

Sin was already shaking his head. "I heard you cut beards every day."

"I do. But only for customers."

Sin laughed, and pulled a wad of yellow banknotes out from inside his coat pocket. He began putting $50 notes on the counter. "I always pay my way." He glanced up. "How many of these do I need to become a customer?"

Joffa clenched his fists around the handles of his crutches. "What did I tell you, fella? Your dirty money is not welcome here."

"Really? Your marshmallow-soft mate Moose might disagree. I heard he was all in favour of selling the whole museum to me."

Joffa turned red and spluttered. "Who told you that?"

"I have ways of finding out things. Anyway, my money is not dirty.

It came with the church. Who knew they'd forget to empty the poor box?" He made a tut-tutting noise. "Finders keepers, that's always been my motto."

"You expect us to believe that? People who donate to poor boxes wouldn't put in $50 notes."

"What can I say? It's hard to understand how the meek expect to inherit the earth when they're so busy giving it away."

Katy smirked at him. "I only cut the beard of one lucky customer a day, and as you can see …" She pointed to the German in the chair.

"OK, I'll come back tomorrow."

"You have to be on one of the tour buses, fella," Joffa said.

Rod weighed in. "If you're standing outside the church around noon, I'll pick you up."

Joffa and Katy looked at him.

"What?" Rod said. "What did I say? Five minutes ago you were fine with me bringing bearded men here by any means."

"Not this fella though," Joffa said.

"Why not?" Rod said.

"Yes, why not me?" Sin said.

Joffa rolled his eyes. "I'm warning you, fella. You don't want to get in a war with Moose and me."

"I've met men like you before. All bluff. But you're really as weak as water. What's an invalid like you realistically expecting to do to me?"

"You won't be talking so calmly after I stick one of these crutches up your clacker."

"Oh charming, I wouldn't be in a hurry to get rid of your crutches if I were you. You're going to need them both if your legs somehow get broken."

"Are you threatening me?"

"If that's the way you interpret it …" Sin smiled. "So, where is your doppleganger?"

Katy and Joffa looked at each other. "He's busy doing some work in the shed," Joffa lied.

"Really?" Sin made another tut-tutting noise. "Only, I heard he's gone bush with that scruffy little American."

"What makes you think that?" Joffa said. "Besides, he's the least of your problem. You've heard of Big Jake, have you?"

Sin made the tut-tutting noise again, then addressed Rod. "I take it you are leaving with your passengers soon? The place will be *so* empty without you."

Then he addressed Katy and Joffa. "I *will* be back."

————

Sin stormed out.

Fifteen minutes later, Rod left with eight passengers.

Ten minutes later, Joffa and Katy pointed the clean-shaven German backpacker towards Hobart and waved him goodbye.

When they went back inside, Joffa looked at Katy. "How did Sin know those tings?"

"Beats me," Katy said. "I didn't tell him."

Joffa kept staring."I didn't think you did. I'm thinking about Moose though."

"You really think he'd rat out on us like that?"

"We know he has friends with a criminal background."

"And you haven't? You admitted it yourself: this Big Jake is a career criminal."

"Jaysus, but he's like The Equaliser or the A team. If you can find him, he's always on the side of good."

"So you've found him?"

"I didn't say that. But I'm getting closer. I've left messages."

Katy bit her lip. "Don't judge Moose by what he's done in the past is all I'm saying."

"Well, that eejit knew somehow. I know neither of us told him. That just leaves Moose." He rubbed the back of his neck and his facial expression changed. "It's all starting to make sense now."

"What is?" Katy said,

"How well do you know Doc Jenkins?"

"What are you saying? He's been my doctor since I was 13."

"Did you know he used to work at Risdon Prison?"

"How do you know that?"

"He let it slip when he was stitching me up. And guess where Moose was about that time?"

"But Moose told us he doesn't even know him. Even if you're right, how could he have told him he was going bush? Moose made the decision on the spur of the moment."

"He had to pass the surgery on the way to the track, or he might have called him on his mobile phone?"

"But Doc Jenkins? He's so … so … normal."

"Is he? Did they even find George Pickles's body?"

"I never knew they had even lost his body. I went to his funeral."

"You never wondered about the skeleton in Doc Jenkins's rooms? The one he calls George?"

"Nooooo?"

Joffa nodded. "Doc Jenkins might not be the cleanskin you think he is." He paused. "Of course, Tim is the other candidate. Maybe he's trying to keep Moose out there for as long as possible so Sin and his men can attack us."

Katy shook her head. "I can't see that either. Tim has been nothing but loyal to us since he arrived."

"Do you have any better explanations?" Joffa blew out a loud out-take of air. "The good ting is if Sin knows Moose and Tim aren't here, he knows I'm sleeping here. And whatever he says, he is more scared of me than I am of him."

Katy held out her outstretched thumb and forefinger. "I'm this close to calling Stretch."

"To tell him what? That the chap who kindly came to the rescue of the Catholic church is doing what?"

"He's trying to intimidate us."

"Jaysus, Katy. You were the only one armed when he came in asking for a beard trim. He could argue you were the one trying to intimidate him with sharp scissors! Besides, we don't even know what he's after."

· "Isn't it obvious? Gus was right. He's trying to muscle in on the bushranger whiskers business."

"Maybe. You and Moose seem to think that old biker is the Oracle of Delphi."

————

Katy couldn't believe her eyes when the afternoon tour bus pulled into the car park.

"It's an actual bus, not a mini-bus." She hugged Joffa." It's working, it's working, my idea is working."

She could see through the window the driver of the bus was shaking his head, and possibly swearing about all the tradies utes blocking his way. He just pulled up right behind them and cut the engine.

Nine of the 23 customers who filed off the bus were sporting beards but Katy could honestly say none of them were as good as the German backpacker's, which made her feel good about making the early call to make him the daily winner.

The nine bearded blokes all had their heads high as they came through the door, as if to say *pick me, pick me.*

The bus didn't just have a driver. Sally Hopkins was back as tour guide and recognised Joffa when she went up to the reception desk. "Professor O'Brien, you're still here."

"You didn't hear. I'm just Joffa now." He pointed. "This is my wife. Katy, this is Sally Hopkins, the tour owner."

"Pleasure." Katy reached over the counter to shake hands.

"I had to come see for myself," Mrs Hopkins said. "I didn't think you could ever top the last marketing gimmick but this latest one seems to be capturing people's attention, so I had to see it in action for myself."

"Oh." Katy bit her lip. "I'm afraid we've already had a winner today. He was a backpacker on Rod Whish-Willson's bus."

Mrs Hopkins frowned. "Funny? I was at the depot when he left. I don't remember seeing any backpacker."

Mrs Hopkins pinched the bridge of her nose, then nodded towards the nine bearded men, who were now huddled in a group in the corner preening themselves like peacocks. "What am I going to tell them?"

Katy sighed. "I guess I can do one more, but just this once."

———

By the time Katy had cleaned up it was 4pm and she was sharing a pot of tea in the upstairs flat.

"You need to get the two lots of whiskers to Gus," Joffa said.

Katy shook her head. "Why don't I stay here with you tonight? I have something very special to share with you."

"Oh Moose would like that? Both of us naked in his bed? But as much as I like the idea, I'd prefer if you were nowhere near this place."

"I didn't mean that!"

Joffa rubbed the back of his neck. "I don't think it's safe for you to be here."

"I thought you said you weren't worried?"

"I'm not. But if I'm wrong I might not be able to protect you, not until Big Jake arrives to give me a hand." Joffa dropped his head. "He's a difficult man to track down. You drop those bags off at Gus's, then skedaddle home. I've got this."

"You haven't even got two good legs any more."

"No, but I've gained two good weapons." He patted one of the crutches leaning on the wall just behind him. "I don't think for a minute Sin will even come back here tonight, but if he does he can't say I never warned him."

"Aren't you worried he knows I'll be alone? I am. He's bound to know where we live."

"That place is like Fort Knox. He'd need a helicopter to burst into the upstairs windows."

"What if he's already in the house?"

Joffa sighed. "If it makes you more comfortable, I'll come with you and give the flat the once-over to put your mind at rest."

Katy got up and tucked the two bags of whiskers under her arm, and they both headed for the door. As they walked down the hall, she said, "What if Sin sees us leaving? He's got a good view of our front door from the back of the church."

"He'll think twice about breaking into this place when he hears Gough barking."

They descended the stairs and stopped by the door to punch in the alarm code.

"Thanks for doing this," Katy said. "It means we can talk on the walk into town."

Joffa's expression turned solemn. "I'm not angry with you any more, if dat's what you're worried about."

"What?"

"I'm past being cranky about you wasting money by going to the doctor. It's just I'm under stress worrying where the money is coming from, and with all the tings happening."

Katy's mouth fell open.

She said barely a word on the way home.

————

When he had delivered Katy to Gus's office, Joffa went across the road to the flat and searched it from room to room.

He looked under every bed, which was no mean feat when he was using crutches, and he opened every large wardrobe and cupboard.

When Gus walked Katy back and she invited him in for a cuppa, Joffa was able to inform her no one was hiding in the flat.

"Who were you expecting?" Gus said as he nursed his cup on one side of the red-speckled formica table in the tiny kitchenette.

Joffa had leaned his crutches up against the kitchen sink and squeezed his way across the bench inch by inch until there was enough room for Katy to sit beside him. "You know Sin's partner has bought the building site next to the museum. And Sin has bought the Catholic Church on the other side?"

Gus threw his head into his hands. "Oh, this is bad. Real bad."

"You heard, too, about the dwarf that was kidnapped?" Joffa said.

Gus shook his head. "I didn't know we even had any dwarfs in Windy Mountain."

"Not human ones," Katy said. "Someone stole a concrete one from a garden up on High Street. Executed him, too, with a concrete cutter."

Joffa said, "Katy isn't so sure, but I think it was one of the workmen from the construction site."

"Really? So it's not only the Bushranger Whiskers business they're after? What does Moose think of all this?" Gus said.

"We're not even sure which side Moose is on," Joffa said.

Gus looked from face to face. "Hang on! What are you saying?"

"We're not saying anyting, but Sin knows stuff that only Moose could know, so how else could he get that information?"

Gus continued staring. "I've known Moose for a lot longer than you, Joffa, and no way would he betray youse. There has got to be another explanation. Have you asked him?"

"We can't," Joffa said. "He's gone bush."

Gus drained his cup but he didn't look like someone enjoying it. "I'm out of here." He sucked in his stomach, slid to the end of the bench seat, stood up awkwardly and waved a finger. "I thought you people were his friends. I'll show myself out."

When the door slammed shut downstairs, Joffa asked Katy to move so he could slide out, too.

"I'd better be getting back to the museum," he said.

———

The glow of the clock-radio on the bedside cabinet told Joffa it was nearly midnight.

He was sleeping in Tim's bed again. Katy had made it up with crisp, fresh sheets while he was out seeing Doc Jenkins.

But his throbbing foot had kept him awake for nearly two hours despite him washing down the painkillers the doctor had prescribed him.

It's very hard to toss and turn when you have a sore and bandaged foot.

But your bladder doesn't care about your immobility. All it cares about is you drank all that water, and when you've got to go, you've got to go.

This is why Joffa carefully slid out of bed, grabbed one crutch from its resting place against the wall and hopped like Long John Silver in only his underpants out the door. Only the light that came through the window guided his way towards the bathroom. He closed the door through habit rather than need for privacy.

When he re-emerged, he realised immediately the hall light was on. Then he heard whistling and the footsteps of someone coming up the stairs.

Joffa leant against the wall and shimmied to the end. Heel, slide, toe, slide. Then he raised his crutch.

When the intruder came around the corner, and saw the crutch about to come crunching down on his head, he gasped.

"You weren't supposed to be here, Joffa."

———

"How do you know I wasn't supposed to be here?" Joffa lowered the crutch when he realised podgy little Dave Jenkins posed no threat.

"Mr Sin told me." The undertaker's voice dropped to a nervous whisper and his eyes fell on the closed door to the lounge. "Keep your voice down, for God's sake. I don't want him to hear us?"

Joffa looked at the door, too, then looked the intruder in the eye. "Don't tell me he has the place bugged?"

"I shouldn't be telling you this." Dave's voice started to crack. "But he made me put a microphone behind the books." He wiped a tear rolling down his left cheek. "He said if I didn't do what he said, I'd end up in one of my own caskets and he knew exactly where to hide my body."

Joffa rubbed the back of his neck. It made sense to him now. He knew Dave knew the alarm code, and Gough was so used to his scent he no longer wasted any energy growling.

"How did Sin know you even had access to this place?"

"Mr Sin found out from my father. But it's not what you think. Dad hadn't seen him for years, he came here to get away from men like Sin."

"But he told him about you and the books?"

"Mr Sin can be very persuasive." He paused. "The speaker worked fine at first and Mr Sin said he heard every word crystal clear."

So that's how he knew Moose was in favour of selling? He was eavesdropping on their meeting.

"But something happened to dislodge the listening device," Dave said. "That's why I'm here, to see if I can get it working again. Mr Sin said he saw you and Katy lock up and go home for the night."

"And you believed him?"

"You don't question a man like Mr Sin. Have you met him? He's one scary dude."

"Oh, I've met him all right. And if he wants to eavesdrop we'd better make sure he has something good to listen to."

SIX
IT'S NOW OR NEVER

KATY DECIDED on her walk to work there was no point trying to talk to Joffa if he didn't want to listen to her. So she was not even going to try to deliver the good news, and keep conversation to a cool minimum.

But he disarmed her as soon as she entered the foyer. "You wouldn't believe it? We did have an intruder last night."

"Are you hurt?" Katy raced to the counter to see if he had any bruising on his face.

Joffa looked back blankly from the other side. "From that little fella? Are you kidding?"

"What Mr Sin lacks in height he makes up for in girth."

"But it wasn't actually Sin. It was Dave Jenkins."

Katy walked to the gate, and lifted it. She put her handbag down on one of the shelves below the counter and looked at Joffa searchingly.

"Turns out that Sin pressured Dave into hiding a listening device behind the sci-fi books," he said.

Katy gasped as she stopped in front of him. "He was bugging us?"

Joffa nodded. "The good news is I reckon I set it on the blink when

I threw that book at our meeting with Moose. The bad news is Sin caught most of the conversation."

"So that's how he knew Moose wanted to sell? It wasn't Moose or Tim or Doc Jenkins after all. That lifts the veil of suspicion on them."

Joffa shook his head. "It doesn't get Doc Jenkins off the hook. He was the one who told Sin about the books. No telling what else he told him."

"But Moose is in the clear?"

"You really think we should trust him again? We already know he has no sense of loyalty."

"But Tim's OK surely?" Katy said.

"Depends what you mean by OK. In my mind, he's still an eejit."

She smiled. "So what have you done with the listening device?"

"I relocated it."

"Where to?"

"You don't want to know! All I'll say is Sin will have some difficulty interpreting what he hears from the other end from now on. I told Dave to report back to Sin that it should be working fine now."

"How can you be sure he'll do that?"

"I told him he'd have me to contend with if he didn't. It's a question of who scares him the most, and I think I'm out front of Sin."

———

Joffa was leaning on his crutches looking up at the sign that stretched across the space above the windows. It read *Windy Mountain Tasmanian Tiger Museum.*

Katy just didn't appreciate the difficulty of condensing the type to squeeze *Windy Mountain Tasmanian Tiger and Bushranger Whiskers Museum* in the same space. Even worse, how would he even be able to get up there on a ladder in his state?

When he realised gravel was being kicked up behind him, he turned to see a familiar mini-bus parked amid all the tradies utes, and Wash-Wish waving to him from the driver's seat with a big, silly grin.

Next eight little men with beards stepped down from the bus, and a beaming Wash-Wish alighted in his sky-blue blazer, green shorts and odd socks — one white and one bigger yellow one.

"Ta da," Wish-Wash's grandson said as he approached him. "Don't say I never deliver!" Then he squinted at Joffa. "How did you hurt your leg?"

Joffa threw his right-hand crutch to the ground and wrapped his arm around Wash-Wish. He turned him around so no one could hear them, and whispered. "Are these little fellas who I think they are?"

Wash-Wish returned his frown. "I thought you'd be pleased I brought someone other than Sin."

"You're not going to tell me they were all hitch-hiking too?"

"No, this lot is legit. I picked them up at the depot in Launceston. They're performing at the Princess Theatre from next week."

Joffa spun around. "But there are eight of them?" he said out of the side of his mouth. "Is one of them supposed to be Snow White?"

Wash-Wish rolled his eyes. "You know actors? One of them is always breaking a leg. So one is an understudy." He watched Joffa's face change. "I expected you to be more excited. I'm sure Katy will share my enthusiasm."

"You do know you're wearing odd socks?"

"You noticed?" Wash-Wish whistled to himself. "I thought I was getting away with it."

"No one has noticed?"

"No one has said anything."

———

"What the fuck is going on?" came a booming voice from the other side of the building site.

Joffa turned to see Moose approaching, carrying a backpack.

When Moose drew to a halt in front of him, he said, "Who the hell are these little blokes?"

Wash-Wish scowled at him. "These little *actors* have ears, you know! And feelings! How would you like it if they bellowed in your earshot: 'Who the hell are these two giants?'"

Wash-Wish turned to the dwarfs. "Let's get in out of this sun and leave these politically incorrect ignoramuses out here to fry." He marched them white-yellow, white-yellow to the front door.

When they had gone inside, Moose said, "And what the fuck are you doing with *my* crutches? Looks like you've hurt yourself."

"I trod on some broken mirror upstairs."

Moose laughed. "Who's the clumsy one now?" Then he processed fully what had been said and scowled. "What the fuck were you doing in my bedroom?"

"Someone had to guard the museum with you storming off in a huff, which reminds me: I thought you said you didn't know Doc Jenkins!"

Moose said slowly, "What makes you think I do?"

"Who do you think stitched up my foot?"

Moose let out a loud blast of breath. "So I know him. Big deal! We've even caught up. Is that a crime?"

"Luckily for you, the listening device might have saved your bacon."

Moose frowned. "What listening device?"

"The one Sin planted in the lounge upstairs."

"Fucking oath! How did he do that?"

"Long story," Joffa said. "You wouldn't believe some of the stuff dat's been going on around here."

Moose scratched his thickening stubble. "It hasn't been a barrel of laughs for me either."

Joffa realised who was missing now. "Where's Tim?"

Moose turned and Joffa followed. Tim was shuffling this way, carrying an even heavier-looking backpack than the one he had when he left.

———

When the scraggly bearded Texan put down his rattling backpack and pulled out a handkerchief to mop his sweaty brow, Moose snarled. "You tell him, Awesome Sauce."

"Tell him *what*?" Tim said, between puffs.

"Tell him what you did with all the toilet paper you carried up the mountain."

Joffa's eyes widened. "You took the museum's toilet paper supplies?"

"Not all of it."

"Just tell him what you did with it," Moose bellowed.

Tim looked up at him. "I got a good fire going, didn't I?"

Moose turned to Joffa. "Someone — and I'm not mentioning any names — refused to go pick up kindling or logs because it turns out he's scared of snakes. I don't know how you two actually caught *anything*."

"Not this again?" Joffa pinched the bridge of his nose and closed his eyes.

"He nearly pissed his pants when a wallaby came crashing through the bush towards us," Moose said. "And I've never seen someone jump like he did when a kookaburra started laughing on a gum tree overlooking the campsite."

Tim shouted, "OK big shot, tell him what you did to my guitar."

"I didn't do anything to it. It was the fire that burned it."

Joffa opened his eyes. "You burned his guitar?"

Moose counted on his fingers. "One: if he had gathered some firewood like I asked, we wouldn't even he having this conversation. Two: if he hadn't pulled the guitar out and started singing cowboy songs around the campfire we wouldn't even be having this conversation."

Tim screeched, "You didn't have to wrench it out of my hands and throw it on the fire!"

"No?" Moose said. "The alternative would have been to wrap it around your head and bury you in a shallow grave on Bing Bong Mountain. How would you have felt about that?"

"Well!" Tim said. "Wait till I tell Miss Kate what you just said. I expect Officer Stretch will want to hear it, too? You heard him, Joffa? He threatened to kill me!"

Joffa shook his head and pointed to his bandaged foot. "Do you know how I did this, Tim?"

Tim looked from face to face. "Hang on, I wasn't even here."

"The piece of glass you left in the carpet was though."

They watched as Tim picked up his backpack, grunting as he wrestled it on to his back again.

He stumbled towards the door like a wobbly weightlifter.

When he disappeared inside, Joffa said, "If he hasn't got the bog paper in there, or his guitar, what's weighing him down?"

"Shells," Moose said.

"What kind of shells?"

"They looked like sea-shells to me."

"Are you kidding me? Bing Bong Mountain is miles away from the sea."

"We found these ones scattered at the entrance to a cave."

"And Tim collected them. Why?"

"He seems to fancy himself as some kind of David Attenborough. I lost count of how many shells he put up to his ear. He put on a faux Texan voice. *I really can hear the sea in this one*?"

"I bet that went down well with you?"

"I told him he was on his own carrying them. But he said he had an idea to help the museum and he didn't want to share the glory with a guitar vandal like me anyway. I told him if that's the way he felt about it, I definitely wouldn't help him. Serves the little bastard right if he can't walk straight tomorrow."

They both laughed, and Joffa brought Moose up to date on what had been going on, starting with how Sin thought Moose was a pussy who would back down easily when he started tightening the screws. He also told him about the latest load of shite from the old blokes.

———

Wash-Wish was sitting at a table in the corner dunking a biscuit into his tea when Joffa and Moose came inside. Katy was sliding the makeshift barber's chair into position.

Joffa slumped into the first empty chair he came to.

Moose kept walking towards her. "Did you miss me, Kazza?"

She eyed him with disdain. "I told you you'd be back sooner rather than later?"

"Nothing to do with my foot though." He glanced at Joffa, who was nursing his crutches. "Remind me to leave Awesome Sauce home next time."

"Tim tells me you threatened to kill him."

"The problem with that boy is he can't take a joke. Where is he anyway?"

"He's traumatised. I think he's hiding from you in the toilet upstairs."

"Traumatised, be buggered. He's been holding it in the entire time. I doubt we'll see him for a while." He breathed out loudly. "Still bringing the museum into disrepute, I see, Kazza?"

Katy took her scissors out of her bag and placed them on the table next to the comb and razor.

"It won't do you any good." Moose shook his head. "Wash-Wish has sold you a pup this time. If these little guys are who I assume they are, none of them will want to part with their beards."

"Not all the seven dwarfs have beards, Moose." Joffa waved one of his crutched to add gravitas to his point.

"Pig's arse."

"Joffa's right," Wash-Wish said quickly. "Dopey is clean-shaven."

"Hey, you're right, smart-arses." Moose pointed towards the ceiling. "We have our very own Dopey here. He might actually have grown a beard by the time he comes out of the dunny though."

Katy harrumphed. "So, is it true you threatened him outside?"

Moose looked at Joffa. "Did you hear me threaten him?"

Joffa shook his head.

Katy pinched her left eyebrow. "What's brought you two together again?"

Moose's look darkened. "Joffa was filling me in outside about the things Sin has been saying about me behind my back. I still think you're waving a red rag to a bull by cutting whiskers out in the open, but Sin can go to buggery if he thinks he can call me marshmallow man and get away with it."

Joffa nodded. "We've agreed I still should get Jake over here to help us if I can. Fight fire with fire. Right Moose?"

Moose smacked a fist into his palm. "Wong and Sin will rue the day they challenged us."

"Does this mean you're both harmonising well enough to resume making the concrete dwarf?" Katy asked.

The big men looked at each other.

Joffa shrugged. "I suppose so." He looked down at his bandaged foot. "I'm not going anywhere else for a while."

"I am." Moose pointed towards the downstairs gents. "I can't wait for Awesome Sauce to vacate upstairs any longer."

He headed across the room and disappeared into the washroom.

Katy put her hands on her hips. "Charming! I didn't get the chance to tell him about the other task I had for you guys."

"Another task?" Joffa said. "Can't it wait?"

"Not really," Katy said. "Did you see all the shells Tim brought back? He thinks they are from an Aboriginal midden."

Joffa frowned.

"Middens are places the debris from eating shellfish has accumulated over time," she explained.

Joffa lowered his voice. "Where's this going?"

"We're going to put them on display."

"In the museum? Jaysus, this is a Tasmanian Tiger museum!"

Katy shook her head. "We're going for diversity, remember? It's a good thing you hadn't got around to amending the sign."

Joffa rubbed the back of his neck. "Yeah, about that, Katy. I just can't see how it's going to fit with all those words."

"I'm sure the two of you will find a way. Only now you'll have to make it *The Windy Mountain Tasmanian Tiger, Bushranger Whiskers and Aboriginal Midden Museum.*"

Joffa felt sick. Two more long words!

But that was nothing next to the feeling that came over him when it dawned on him what Moose had just walked into.

———

The last thing Moose expected to see when he came out ten minutes later were the Eight Dwarfs.

One of them was in the barber's chair with a rainbow-coloured bib draped around him as Kazza snipped away.

Wash-Wish was still sitting at the same table, only now he was surrounded by the rest of the dwarfs holding cups and saucers, and looking very grim.

"Christ! You blokes weren't in there for long," Moose said.

"What do you expect?" Wash-Wish said. "There wasn't a whole lot for them to see. The displays were mostly above their eye levels. We were just discussing where we can register our complaint."

Before Moose could reply, Joffa threw up his hands. "Please tell me you didn't use Cubicle Two?"

Moose looked at the pale Irishman. "You know I *always* use Cubicle Two. It has the best graffiti."

"I expect that's down to you."

"You can't prove that!"

Joffa looked at his feet. "Some new evidence may have come to light that does just that."

"Eh?"

The Irishman raised his head and looked Moose in the eyes. "You know I was filling you in on things outside?"

Moose spoke slowly. "Ye-ess."

"And you know I told you about the listening device I relocated."

"What are you trying to tell me?"

Joffa nodded. "I'm afraid I relocated it to Cubicle Two."

————

Joffa looked up at Katy hoping for sympathy. She had stopped her snipping now and returned his look with interest. Her glare seemed to say: You did *what?*

Goodness knows what the Eight Dwarfs thought? They looked around at each other.

When Moose broke into a smile, the tension subsided like a deflating balloon darting and farting around the room. The dwarfs resumed their chattering, Katy went back to work with her scissors.

"You're not angry?" Joffa said above the rising noise.

"It's exactly the kind of thing I would have done." Moose's smile became even broader. "If Sin wants to eavesdrop on us, the least we can do is give him something interesting to hear."

Joffa still felt guilty. "I should have warned you. I really thought only random strangers would ever use that cubicle. I forgot you use it, too."

"Don't beat yourself up. Save that for me to do to you on the chess board."

Joffa felt the colour returning to his face. "Is that so! Don't think I'll fall for the same dirty trick again?"

"No? We'll see."

Joffa pointed to the gents with one of his crutches.

"Will you watch where you're waving that thing." Katy pointed her scissors at him.

"Sorry," Joffa said. "I just want to emphasise what a near miss we've had." He engaged Moose's eyes. "It's just lucky that you didn't use your phone in there."

"Who said I didn't?" Moose smiled like someone in a toothpaste commercial. "I had to call Gus, so he could help me suss out what was happening?"

Joffa banged his head repeatedly on the side of a crutch. "Why? Why? Why?"

"I wanted to find out if Gus knew anything about this Big Jake of yours."

Joffa raised his head again. "Don't you trust my judgement?"

"Nothing wrong with a second opinion."

"Like the one you got from Doc Jenkins?"

Moose raised his palms at Katy, who was now gliding a razor over her client's face. "I know I said I didn't know him — but it was so long ago, Kazza, I didn't even recognise his name at first. But Doc and I go way back so who better to ask when I needed someone to give me the medical all-clear?"

Katy lifted the razor and just looked at him blankly.

Moose turned Joffa's way. "You'll back me up, won't you cobber? Tell Kazza how I really have changed my mind about wanting to sell the museum."

"Ting is I'm not sure I can do that this soon," Joffa said. "You could be up to more of your tricks."

"Christ, what do I have to say?" Moose put his hands on his hips. "Doesn't your discovery of the bug put me in the clear? If I wasn't on your side, why would I even bother asking for Gus's help?"

Joffa shook his head. "So what did Gus say about Big Jake anyway?"

"He's never heard of him. But he did say something about the old guys' flight of fancy in Ireland that might set the cat among Sin's pigeons."

"Jaysus, Moose, what didn't you tell him?"

"He's known Wish-Wash and Oodles nearly for as long as I have and he's a skilled professional advice giver."

"But he's a *financial* adviser!"

"That's the beauty of it. I could just about hear his eyes rolling over the phone but Sin's not to going to know he didn't mean it seriously."

"What did he say?"

"Only that if the old blokes have found a Tasmanian Tiger in Donegal, this museum is going to be worth millions."

————

A voice came from the stairs. "Did you say millions?"

All eyes turned to the source of the Texan twang and the waft of aftershave.

Tim had wet hair from his shower and his face wasn't even trying to grow a beard any more.

"Tim!" Katy gasped as he came down the last steps. "Where are your whiskers?"

He stopped and took hold of the rails. "Moose was right. I looked like a dork when I looked in the shaving mirror."

"He said that?" Katy glared at Moose. "He was nearly ready for harvesting, how could you say that?"

"Have you ever heard me use the word *dork*?"

"What did you call him?"

"Cowboy Bumfluff, nothing worse. This time, anyway."

"It doesn't matter," the American said. "I've decided to go with the clean-shaven look now I've discovered all those shells. I doubt the journalists will want to interview someone looking like I did."

Moose glanced at Joffa. "What did I tell you? Awesome Sauce is going for the David Attenborough look."

Tim frowned. "Who's he?"

"He's the one who inspired you to collect all those shells, Isn't he? You must have seen him on TV?"

"Oh yes, I'm the one who watches too much TV?"

"Are you saying I do?" Moose said.

"Are you kidding? You've always got it on when you're upstairs."

Moose looked around defensively. "I like to keep in touch with what's going on."

"Really?" Tim said. "Which of the Rocky movies keeps you right on top of world affairs?"

Moose gave him his darkest look. "I'd be very, very careful if I were you. And I wouldn't get carried away with all those shells. You'd need a proper anthropologist to confirm how old they are."

"Flapdoodle!"

Moose's mouth twisted. "*Flapdoodle*? What kind of word is that?"

"You said it yourself." Tim said. "The shells will make us millions."

"When did I say that?"

"Just now, when I came downstairs."

Moose blew deeply. "You've got the wrong end of the stick. You came in at the end of the conversation! I wasn't talking about that. I was talking about funny dunny business."

"Funny dunny business?" Tim spoke it slowly like he was speaking a foreign language.

"Well, not so-secret dunny business, as a matter of fact."

Tim stood at the bottom of the stairs frowning.

Katy removed the smock from the understudy and brushed some loose hair from his clothes. "We'll explain later, Tim. So what have you done with your whiskers?"

"A strong wind came up and blew them off his face is what I reckon," Moose mumbled.

Katy gave him another withering look.

"If you must know," Tim said. "I flushed them down the sink."

"Oh great," Joffa said. "Just what we need! A blocked pipe to add to this museum's financial woes!"

———

Joffa saw Katy hand Wash-Wish a brown envelope just before he climbed into the driver's seat.

He was leaning on his crutches at the edge of the car park, so he couldn't hear what she said to him.

Tim was inside the gallery arranging his shells and Moose was having a rare stint behind the computer. It seemed really odd he had volunteered for that job, but perhaps this was evidence he really wanted to be part of the team.

Katy waved goodbye as Wash-Wish backed out and the mini-bus turned on to the road. When she turned and walked towards him, Joffa said, "Did you just give him money?"

"You think I'd give him an empty envelope?"

"Where'd you get it?" He was trembling.

"From the petty cash drawer."

Joffa gripped his crutches tightly. "That's why you went behind the counter! Jaysus, how much did you give him?"

"Only enough to give him an incentive to keep bringing us clients. We'll still make a good profit."

"Is that so? Your friend Gus only pays us at the end of the month. If it's good enough to us to wait, why can't Wash-Wish do the same?"

"My friend Gus? He's as much your friend?"

Joffa waved one of his crutches. "Oh no, you can't pin that on me. You know I've never been a fan."

"Moose is."

"That makes it all right then, does it? Let me remind you Moose was keen to sell this museum to hoods two days ago, which tells me his judgement isn't that great."

"But he's back on board with us now. Isn't he?"

"Maybe. But he doesn't know you just gave heaven knows how much money to Wish-Wash's grandson! Jaysus, Katy, Moose would have a fit if he knew the profits were flying out the door."

"It wasn't that much."

Joffa rubbed the back of his neck. "Did you notice how many biscuits Wash-Wish ate? And did you see how few of the cups of tea around the room were actually finished? That's our money you're pouring down the drain! Again!"

Joffa watched her storm inside.

———

By the time he picked his way inside, Katy was no where to be seen.

Joffa looked around the room but all he saw were empty chairs and tea cups on side tables. "Where'd she go?"

Moose pointed to the ladies. "What did you say to her? She looked like she was crying when she came in."

"I didn't say anything to make her cry."

"Don't give me that. I saw you out the window. You were so angry you were waving one of your crutches at her."

Joffa blew out a stream of air. "So they're *my* crutches now? I thought they were *your* crutches?"

"Oh, no." Moose waved a finger. "Don't try to transfer the blame to me. *You* married her, *you* just said something to upset her, *you* deal with it!"

Joffa swung across the room and started picking up cups awkwardly and transferring them to a single table. "I don't suppose you can give me a hand?"

"Can't you see I'm busy?"

"You? Busy? I thought the computer brought you out in a rash!" He pointed the left crutch towards the gallery. "I thought even helping Tim would be preferable to you."

"You reckon? You try going bush with Awesome Sauce for a whole night and see if you want to arrange sea-shells with him!"

"Please yourself." Joffa hobbled to the next table, muttering. "I don't know why she served tea in those big cups to those dwarfs anyway."

"Can we have some shush?" Moose said. "I'm trying to concentrate here."

Joffa looked over and saw Moose was staring at the screen. By the sound of it, he was typing one finger at a time. *Clunk* …. pause … *clunk* … pause. "Where's the fucking 'a' on this fucking keyboard?"

"Same place it is on all keyboards. Middle line, on the left."

Moose looked down, then he looked up. "How did you know that?"

"Why am I not surprised you never did keyboard lessons at your prison."

"You must be joking! Who does keyboard lessons in the clink?"

"They didn't want to prepare you for a job outside?"

Moose shook his head. "The most useful stuff I learned was about inside jobs, and that was mainly from other inmates." He smiled at the thought then went back to typing. *Clunk …* pause *… clunk …* pause. "These fucking keys were designed for midgets' fingers."

Joffa picked his way back to the front of the counter. "What are you trying to write?"

"If must know, I'm writing an email."

"You've never written an email in your life!"

"That's how much you know. Anyway, this email is important for the well-being of this museum. I'm replying to the old blokes to give them the benefit of my experience in securing the Tasmanian Tiger that's trapped in their kitchen."

"Are you as crazy as they are? Katy and I thought the best strategy was to ignore them."

"But can't you see? If Sin managed to plant a bug upstairs, chances are he's hacked this computer, too. We need to make him believe we're carrying on normally and we don't suspect anything."

"You think he'll think dat's normal behaviour?" Joffa's voice dropped to a whisper.

"You got a better idea?"

———

"What's going on?" Katy said when she came out of the ladies and saw the back of Joffa between two crutches.

He turned around. "What makes you think something is going on?"

"You guys never whisper."

Joffa turned around to Moose. "We weren't whispering, were we?"

"Talking softly maybe."

"That's it." Joffa didn't have to turn far because Katy was beside him at the counter now. "We were discussing the best way to proceed with the construction of the dwarf for the le Blancs."

"You really expect me to believe that?" Her normal course of action would be to eyeball the men to try to detect if they were lying, but she knew to do so would reveal her red, puffy eyes. They had probably guessed she had gone in there for a cry, but they couldn't know for sure. She had pulled herself together now. Whatever they were up to, they obviously weren't going to tell her. Maybe she could get them away from the computer so she could check the browser's history? She looked out the window towards the letter box at the edge of the car park. "Have either of you checked to see if the postie has been?"

"It's a Saturday," Joffa said.

"He might be working over-time."

"I would have noticed if the postie had been," Moose said.

"You might have been distracted by the phone?"

Moose shook his head. "The phone never rang."

"Maybe the postie came early today, and we all missed him?"

Their eyes turned when they heard the swinging of the gallery door.

"All done, Tim?" Katy asked.

He nodded as he pulled up on the other side of Joffa. "I didn't have room for all of them but I think you'll like what I've done."

"I won't," Moose growled. "I've never heard of such a dumb idea."

Katy glared at him. "It's called diversification."

"What's wrong with sticking to our core business, Kazza?"

"Caught any Tasmanian Tigers lately, have you?"

Moose tapped the tip of his index finger on the counter and raised his voice. "How could I? Bad enough I was out of action for so long. When I finally get back to the field, my *partner* puts most of his efforts into collecting fucking sea-shells!"

"Partner?" Tim said, glaring back. "If you were a true partner, you would have helped carry them?"

"I wasn't about to desecrate a sacred Aboriginal site!"

Now Katy chanced eye-to-eye contact with Moose. "Do you really have to swear? And they're shells, not burial bones," she said.

"Doesn't matter. We should have got an expert up there to check them out before disturbing them."

"Since when have you been so culturally sensitive?"

"Why don't you ask the Mayor that some time?"

Katy squinted at him. "James Northan's going to act as a referee for *you*? After what you did to *him*?"

"The point is why did I do to him what I did? Go on, ask him."

"Oh yes? That's going to happen, especially when he's on the other side of the world." Katy held his glare. "You know the old blokes say they've cornered a Tasmanian Tiger in Donegal?"

"Yeah, Joffa told me." Moose broke away from Katy's eyes to exchange glances with the Irishman.

"We think they're just pulling our legs because you told them we were selling the museum?" Katy said.

"So Joffa said."

Katy sighed. "We've decided not to even take the bait. Act as if they'd never said anything."

Moose and Joffa exchanged glances again.

"Let's all take a look at your shell collection, Tim?" Katy looked up to her husband. "Joffa and Moose are going to paint us a new sign on the front facade. It's going to say *The Windy Mountain Tasmanian Tiger, Bushranger Whiskers and Aboriginal Midden Museum.*"

"Really?" the Texan said. "You might decide to reorder the words when you've seen what I've done."

———

Katy sent Tim out to check the letterbox.

When she led Joffa and Moose into the gallery, her first words were, "What the . . . ?"

"Fuck," Moose added.

They stood near the entrance in stunned silence.

Every cabinet in the gallery was now full of sea-shells on beds of green felt. Tasmanian Tiger artefacts that had been in the cabinets were stacked in a pile in the corner, next to the backpack Tim had used to cart the shells in.

The door swung open behind them and they turned to see Tim bound through the door like an excited puppy. He handed Katy two envelopes.

"What do you think?" he said.

Moose looked sharply at Katy. "Now do I have permission to kill him?"

Katy closed her eyes. "My fault, Tim. I should have been more specific. When I said you could use the cabinets, I thought you'd understand I meant the two *empty* cabinets."

"But there's not enough room for the best shells?"

Joffa waved a fist at him. "You'd better put them back before Wish-Wash's grandson sees them and tells the old fella the other exhibits are gone."

"All of the shells?"

"Except for ones in the two cabinets that were already empty," Katy said.

Tim looked from face to face.

"And I want my backpack back — empty and clean," Joffa said.

Moose and Joffa followed Katy towards the door.

"You'll find a couple of buckets in the shed." Moose said as he walked out.

Katy stopped halfway across the foyer, and inspected the two envelopes. She groaned when she saw the logo's.

———

"Someting wrong?" Joffa said as he drew alongside her.

She sighed. "I hope they aren't what I think they are?"

"What do you think they are?"

"Bills."

"We've only just taken over!"

Katy bit her bottom lip as she resumed crossing the foyer and lifted the gate.

Joffa and Moose headed to the front of the counter, and watched her sit down behind the computer. Her face was obscured but the scrunching of paper told Joffa she was opening one of the envelopes.

Then silence.

Moose and Joffa looked at each other.

More ripping.

More silence.

Moose and Joffa looked at each other again.

"So they *are* bills?" Joffa finally said.

"One from the energy company, one from the insurance company," came the muffled reply.

Joffa lent over the counter and saw Katy's face was buried in her hands. The letters and screwed-up envelopes were lying on the table in front of her.

"How much?" Joffa said.

Katy held them out.

Joffa ripped them from her hand and examined the first, then the second. "Jaysus! They don't miss you, do they?"

"It's part of the cost of doing business," Katy said.

"We've only been in fecking business for a week or two. Oodles and Wish-Wash must have known these were about to arrive."

"You know what it's like embarking on a big trip? I don't think bills were even on their mind."

"Yeah, don't be too harsh on them," Moose said.

"Harsh?" Joffa examined Moose's face. "You were ready to sell them down the river two days ago."

"I was, wasn't I?" Moose gazed into the middle distance. "But can't you see I've come around to your way of thinking. No one calls me soft as marshmallow and gets away with it."

"Have you seen the size of these bills?" Joffa waved them in

Moose's face. "Where do you think we're going to get that kind of money?"

He turned the papers back towards himself and examined each of them again. The payments were due by the end of the month.

Moose frowned. "Why do we even need insurance anyway?"

"You have a short memory. If a single thug like Messerschmitt can burn down the pub next door, what mayhem can two thugs wreak? And we don't even know who's really behind the dwarf beheading?" Joffa paused. "Well, we do. The le Blancs think it's down to their son. But since he's been in Risdon for a very long time, he must be getting outside help."

Moose stared into space again. "Funny! I thought I knew all the long-termers in Risdon. You'd think I'd remember anyone with a ponsy name like le Blanc."

"Memory loss is quite common for someone your age."

"Who are you calling old?"

"Guys!" Katy shouted. "Stop this before it gets out of hand again. Your bickering isn't helping anyone."

"He started it," Moose moaned. "I was just sticking up for the old blokes. I'm not the one who's lost my bottle."

"Really?" Joffa said. "Who was the person who stayed here to guard the museum last night ON HIS OWN?"

Moose tapped his own chest. "You won't be needed tonight. I can take care of it. Anyone would think we're under siege from an army." He held up two fingers. "There's only two of them."

"Have you forgotten the gnome beheader?"

"That might just be kids."

"You think? Where would kids get their hands on a concrete cutter?"

"It doesn't matter anyway. It's nothing to do with us."

"You don't think we haven't been dragged into it because Stretch has been using our computer!"

Moose stared. "How would they know?"

"It's a computer. Nothing can actually be erased."

"Nothing?" Moose had the look of panic on his face.

Joffa shook his head. "Nope. Not even the email you sent to the old blokes."

"You sent them an email!" Katy said.

"Can you really see what I wrote?"

She turned her attention to the computer. After just a few keystrokes she looked up at Moose. "You didn't even delete the email trail!"

Katy rolled her eyes and looked back at the screen.

Her face did contortions as she read. "Oh, Moose! How could you?" She addressed Joffa. "Can you even buy honey in Donegal?"

Joffa shrugged. "I never even saw the email so I have no idea what you're talking about."

Moose puffed out his chest. "Clever, eh? If it confuses Katy, imagine what it'll do to Sin?"

"Sin? How did he get into this conversation?" Katy said.

"Moose thinks he might have hacked our computer," Joffa said.

Katy locked eyes with Moose. "And what makes you think that?"

"Simple. If Sin bugged us, he probably has the ways and means to hack us." He pointed to the computer. "That email is really going to do his head in."

"I think it's already doing *my* head in," Katy said.

She followed it to its conclusion, then looked up.

"Why did you have to go and tell them that? *If they trap a Tasmanian Tiger in Ireland it's going to be worth millions?* They won't know you're just pulling their leg!"

The three of them turned when the heard a hiss of brakes.

A bus had pulled up in the car park, and it was a biggun, too. Katy could see lots of heads in the tinted windows.

"Isn't it always the way! We could do with the customers but why do they have to be so early? Quick, Moose, go see how Tim is doing in the gallery."

Moose scowled. "Me? Do you reckon I'm safe to be in the same room as him yet?"

Katy pointed to Joffa's crutches. "Probably not. But you'll be quicker than him."

———

Tim was hunched over a cabinet when Moose burst in with heavy feet and the swing of the door behind him.

The American looked up. "What's the matter?"

Moose looked around. Nothing seemed to have changed. The cabinets were still filled with sea-shells on green felt. "What the fuck have you been doing?"

"It's a lot harder than you think trying to work out what stays and what's expendable. If I was going any faster I'd catch up to tomorrow."

Moose looked skywards. "You're lucky I haven't actually got time to kill you. A big bus has just pulled up and the customers will be expecting to see Tasmanian Tiger stuff. Not your sorry corpse! And definitely not fucking sea-shells. So shift it!"

Tim looked at his watch. "I thought I had more time."

"You haven't. They'll be coming through the front door right now."

"Can't Miss Kate STALL them?"

"How?"

"I don't KNOW. Cut their beards?"

Moose looked back towards the door. "How long do you need?"

"Hmm. Three hours?"

"Three hours?" Moose spat. "It took you much less time to set these up in the first place!"

"That's when I had more room to spread things out. It's much harder when you have to be selective."

"For fuck's sake." Moose shook his large right-hand index finger at Tim. "Half an hour is all you get to put the proper displays back in those cabinets. I'll try to get Kazza to stall them, but no longer than half an hour. Right?"

———

When Moose went back through the door he realised immediately the flaw in the plan.

There wasn't a beard among the many faces that turned his way.

Two men stood over near the counter. One was Joffa, who was leaning on his crutches and talking to a clean-shaven bloke with a big nose who was dressed in the green shorts, blue shirt the tour drivers wore.

The customers standing around in groups all appeared to be women.

Katy was mingling with them and turned when she heard his foot-steps coming close. "Oh there you are, Moose? Is Tim ready for our guests?"

"Ah, not quite." Moose bent down to whisper in her ear.

She looked up to him as if she hadn't quite heard or couldn't believe what she had heard. "How long?"

He mouthed: "Half an hour."

Her eyes narrowed.

Moose shrugged. What could he do?

Katy walked across to the driver, and spoke to him.

The way he was shaking his head didn't look good.

After a bit, he announced loudly, "Can I have your attention, ladies?"

The room fell silent.

"I've just been told there's been a further delay. If I'm going to get you back to your rehearsal on time, I'm afraid we can't hang around."

————

Joffa threw his head into his hands as he realised the significance of this moment. The museum finally had a decent number of customers, only now it didn't. All he could see in his mind's eye were bills, bills, bills and a dwindling income.

He glanced over to Moose who returned a look that had *told-you-Awesome-Sauce-was-a-dickhead-for-bringing-those-shells-home* all over it.

To add salt to the wound, Big Nose had a parting dig at him at the door as he shepherded his passengers towards the bus. "Get well soon. But do pass on my regards to Killer and the other old bloke."

———

"What was that all about, Moose?" Katy demanded as they watched the bus pull out.

"It wasn't my fault," Moose said. "The little shit said he needed three hours to rearrange the sea-shells, I gave him half an hour. We thought you could cut someone's beard. How was I to know they would be all women?"

"They're a visiting forty-woman choir from Melbourne." She turned her focus to Joffa. "And who's Killer?"

"Um, that'll be Oodles. Old story. Long story."

"Spare me the details." Katy lifted the gate and retrieved her handbag from behind the counter.

Joffa watched her head to the door. "Where are you going?"

She stopped and turned. "Home."

"Home? We don't normally go home for lunch?"

"I'm not going home to lunch. I'm going home for the day."

"Oh," Joffa said, trying not to sound surprised. "OK. You should have told me you didn't feel well." He glanced at Moose. "We can cover for you, can't we, Moose?"

"You do know we have one more bus to come?" she said.

"No probs," Joffa said. "See you at home later."

Katy shook her head. "Actually, I'd rather you didn't. I need a night alone."

"What? You heard Moose. He doesn't even want me here tonight."

Katy looked from face to face. "I've had it with you guys today. You. Moose. Tim. Killer. And he's not even here. You all deserve each other."

She turned her machine gun eyes on Moose. "Honey? For goodness sake!" With that, she left, slamming the door behind her.

Joffa watched her opened-mouth through the window until she disappeared from view, then turned to Moose "What did I do?"

"Beats me," Moose said. "She didn't look well to me. I can have a word to Doc Jenkins about her if you like?"

———

Moose and Joffa didn't need Katy's help with the third bus that afternoon.

That's because they had to turn it away again because the gallery still wasn't ready.

It provided a rare chance for Moose to impose his own management style.

He grabbed the back of Awesome Sauce's suspenders, marched him out of the room and told him to stay out if he knew what was good for him.

Then he turfed out the shells himself and replaced them with the Tasmanian Tiger exhibits stacked in the corner.

When Awesome Sauce eventually got to inspect it, his expression gave his feelings away.

But this gave Moose an excuse to wheel out his management skills again. "You don't like it? What are you going to do about it?"

"Why are you so angry at me?" the Texan asked.

"Could it be you're such a fuckup! Name me just one thing you've done right?"

Awesome Sauce looked down at his sneakers. When he looked up, he had tears in his eyes. "You never made a mistake when you were 19? Grand-daddy always told me that's how you learn best — from your mistakes."

SEVEN
A LITTLE LESS CONVERSATION

WHEN KATY SET out on her walk to work just before 8am, she resolved she was going to pretend to be quite upbeat when she reached the museum. When she looked up and saw Sin waiting outside the door, that plan evaporated.

It was Sunday. So the car park was empty of tradies' utes. As Katy came closer to Sin, she glanced through the window hoping to see either Moose or Joffa behind the computer. But the foyer looked empty, too.

She tried to be brave. "If you're here for a beard trim, Mr Sin, you're out of luck. I told you the other day it's for customers only."

Sin smiled, in the manner a cat might look at a mouse at dinnertime. "I'm just keeping my promise. I told you I'd be back."

Katy's hand shook as she inserted the key and turned it. "I'm sure you'll want to meet Moose then. I'll just call him down?"

Sin followed her inside.

"Moose!" she shouted. "We have a guest."

The only sound was her voice. No reply. No creaking floorboards upstairs. *Where were they?*

It was only when she looked over to the couch and saw the empty sleeping bag, she feared the worst. She was all alone.

Sin made no attempt to follow her when she lifted the gate and went to the computer, which was a relief. It meant there was at least a barrier between him and her. He was tall enough to rest his elbow on the front of the counter, but only just.

"I heard Moose was back," Sin said.

"I expect he's upstairs sleeping?" She called again.

Sin made a tut-tutting noise. "How many people stayed here last night?"

"Moose, Joffa and Tim."

"That sounds about right. I saw three men leaving about 10 minutes ago. They weren't walking towards me so I think we can rule out church. Breakfast in town perhaps?"

Of course! Since Gordo had gone to jail and Wendy had been left to run The Wind Tunnel Cafe on her own, she had started opening on Sunday morning in the hope of catching people on their way home from church. But if that's where Moose, Joffa and Tim had gone, service was slow these days — which meant they wouldn't be back for ages.

Sin examined her face and the sweat on her forehead. "You don't look so well. Anything I can do?"

Katy grabbed her water bottle from the desk and sipped it. It was warm and tasted like sardines. Doc Jenkins had warned her morning sickness was just around the corner. But who knew it would kick in this very moment. "Just thirsty," she lied.

Sin squinted at her. "That's good. Because I don't want you getting sick on me. Who would cut the beards when I take over."

Katy summoned up the courage to look Sin in the eye. "You obviously didn't get the message. It's NOT FOR SALE."

"No need to shout at me, Katy. I can call you Katy?"

"No, you can't," came an Irish accent from behind him.

Katy had been too preoccupied to see Joffa, Moose and Tim coming down the street, and Sin had his back to the window, but now they were coming through the doorway, Tim holding the door open for the man with the crutches "It's Mrs O'Fury to you, Sin."

When Sin turned around, Moose said, "So this is the new Holy man next door. I didn't really take in much about him the other day because I was a tad distracted. But you were right, Joffa. He's built like a *little* brick shithouse. Where's his other half?"

Sin smiled. "Big men like you have never scared me. I take the attitude, you see, the bigger they are, the harder they fall."

Now Joffa leaned on his crutches and smiled. "You think we're big? Wait till you see Big Jake?"

"You've tracked him down, have you?" Sin leant back on the counter with the demeanour of someone who was totally relaxed. "Only I heard your friend Gus has never even heard of him."

Moose came over all faux angry. "Where did you hear that?"

"Oh, I have my sources." Sin sighed. "That's why I'm here. I also heard this museum might be worth more than I thought it was, so I'm here to up my offer."

Joffa reacted first. "How much to?"

"How does a million dollars sound?"

Joffa gulped. "One. Zero. Zero. Zero. Zero. Zero, Zero?"

"That's what I said. Interested?"

"No," growled Moose as he stepped towards him.

Sin locked eyes with him. "I thought you were the one who wanted to sell?"

"Who told you that?" Moose barked again.

"I can't reveal my sources."

"Well, they're wrong." Moose thumped a finger repeatedly on Sin's barrel chest. "But my sources are pretty good. I hear you think I'm a pushover. You'd be wise to listen to Kazza. THE MUSEUM IS NOT FOR SALE." He pointed to the door. "Go in peace and not in fucking pieces."

———

As soon as Sin disappeared from sight on the other side of the window, Joffa turned to Moose. "A million dollars! think about how many of our financial problems that would solve?"

"Can't you see?" Moose growled. "This is the evidence we needed Sin *has* hacked our computer. He took the bait!"

"What's wrong with reeling him in then and taking the money?"

"Where do you think a slime-ball like Sin would get a million bucks? If he could lay his greasy paws on it, it would come in crumpled bills of small unmarked notes."

Joffa blew out his cheeks. "Yeah, I guess you're right."

He looked over at Katy, who was nodding.

———

"Am I glad you guys turned up when you did?" Katy said. "I was really scared."

"You can thank Wendy," Tim said. "A sign on the cafe door said to go right in and make ourselves comfortable. We sat down but no one turned up after ten minutes, so here we are."

"Where was she?" Katy's wave of sickness had gone, probably banished by fright.

"Who cares," Joffa said as he wrapped a giant arm around the American. "Not only has Tim volunteered to do the sign writing for us, he says he cooks a mean batch of hotcakes with bacon and maple syrup, and that seems a better deal than what Wendy serves up on a greasy plate anyway."

"I'm only doing it to get my bed back," Tim said. "My spine is killing me."

Katy looked over to the sleeping bag then to Joffa. "Did you make poor Tim sleep on the couch?"

"Nothing of the sort," Moose said. "It was his own choice. Awesome Sauce wasn't in any condition to walk up those stairs last night."

Moose slapped him on the back and Tim winced. "C'mon, you have to go up sooner or later. No pain, no gain."

He turned him towards the stairs.

Katy tried to ignore Tim's yelps with every step as Joffa followed them up on his crutches.

She sifted through the overnight emails.

———

"We tried sliding honey laced with sedatives under the door," the overnight email from Donegal said. "But it didn't work. We can still hear something threshing around in the kitchen. Any other ideas?"

For goodness sake! Katy knew there was no point calling Moose down from upstairs when he had just gone up there with bacon on his mind. The spiral steps had barely stopped vibrating from the three of them climbing at once. Now she could hear feet and crutches disappearing down the hall.

The email was signed by all three of the old men but Wish-Wash's DNA was all over it. Oodles might have gone along with it but if the Mayor ever had a sense of humour, it had been surgically removed at birth.

This joke was getting out of hand.

Should she tell him the truth that Moose was just stringing them along, too, because he wanted to string the hacker along?

They'd never understand that concept. What were hackers to them anyway? The Mayor might think hackers were weekend golfers, but the other two old men wouldn't even get that far with it.

She sighed, undid her hair band and retied her ponytail. *Think, think, think.*

By now, she could smell bacon cooking. That set her stomach churning again.

She was about to dash to the bathroom when the computer started typing on its own.

First the cursor clicked the 'reply' button.

Then the words appeared letter by letter in capitals.

"T R Y V I N E G A R."

————

If the spiral staircase hadn't shuddered so much, Moose and Joffa might have been able to sneak up on her thirty minutes later. But the noise broke her out of her trance, and Katy turned her head to see Moose reach the ground floor first, with Joffa pogoing after him holding his crutches awkwardly. Neither of them looked happy.

When Joffa saw her, he said, "You OK? You look like you've seen a ghost."

"I think I might have done." Katy pointed to the computer screen. "You sure you sent that email on your own, Moose?"

He looked blackly at her. "I said I did, didn't I? Don't you think I'm smart enough to work out how email works?"

"Honey?" she said. "That was your idea? No one else's?"

"I saw him doing it," Joffa said.

"Christ, I only said it to confuse any hackers," Moose said. "Wish-Wash would know I was only pulling his leg."

"We have a bigger problem now. We *are* being hacked but it's worse than just that. I think Sin has remotely taken over the computer."

"How?" Joffa said.

Katy shook her head. "Beats me. All I know is someone sent an email to Donegal pretending to be us and now our keyboard has been locked." She looked around. "Where is Tim? We need to alert the old blokes the email didn't come from us. Tim might know how to regain control?"

"He's washing the dishes upstairs," Joffa said.

"Is that fair? Didn't he cook?"

"We should have waited for Wendy to come back," Moose growled. "At least she'd have eggs."

"He cooked hotcakes without eggs?" Katy locked eyes with him.

"He knew there were *supposed* to be eggs in the mix," Joffa said. "But when he opened the fridge and saw there were none, and no milk either, at least no milk without lumps in it, he didn't seem worried at all. He said vegan hotcakes were actually the latest ting."

"Really? How did it come out?"

"You don't want to know, Katy," Joffa said.

"It looked and smelled like watery vomit on a plate," Moose added.

Katy closed her eyes slowly. Joffa was right. She didn't want to know. "Good thing you had bacon to cover the taste though."

"He burnt it to a fucking cinder," Moose grumbled.

"Good then you had maple syrup?" Katy said.

Moose shook his head. "All he could find in the cupboard was honey. We had plates of vomit and charcoal covered in honey, which we all tipped in the rubbish bin." He started heading for the door with Joffa in tow. "We're off to The Wind Tunnel again. You have my number if anything comes up."

Katy sighed. "I don't know how you can think of eating at a time like this. We've been hacked, for goodness sake. Don't you even want to know what the ghost email said?" Katy cried as they reached the door.

Moose had his hand on the handle but turned around. "Trust me, I think better on a full stomach. So tell us the details when we get back."

"Will Tim be following you there?" Katy said. "I really need to pick his brain about the computer."

"If he does follow us, he can fucking-well sit at the next table," Moose roared. "But I very much doubt any of us will see him anytime soon. I told him to keep scrubbing that pan until he can see his face in it."

Joffa laughed. "I remember buying that pan. It was black when I got it."

"I know." Moose laughed, too.

As soon as they disappeared from sight, Katy dashed to the bathroom.

————

Moose saw them as soon as he entered the cafe.

In the 30 years he had been coming in here, The Wind Tunnel had been through three lots of owners and several coats of paint but it had only ever had room for the same two formica-topped tables.

Doc Jenkins looked up from his conversation when Moose held the door open behind him so Joffa could swing through.

Doc Jenkins put down his mug. "Fancy seeing you both here!"

"I didn't think you did house calls these days?" Moose directed his bellowing voice to the kitchen saloon door. "Who have you poisoned this time, Wendy?"

A blonde middle-aged woman in an apron came through the swinging door and said huskily. "I might have known it was you and your terrible twin." She studied Joffa. "What have you done to yourself, love?"

"I cut my foot on a piece of glass."

Moose opened his mouth to expand on the story, but Wendy waved a finger. "Save it. Just sit down and don't open you gob again till your food arrives."

Moose nodded. "Big servings!"

"What did I just say?" With that, Wendy disappeared out back. Moose assumed she'd scrape dripping into the frying pan before ducking out back to suck the life out of a fag while the pan became hot enough for the black pudding and snags to go in.

Doc Jenkins's companion stood up and offered a hand: "I have you two at a disadvantage. I know who you are but I don't think you know me."

Doc Jenkins said, "Forgive me, I assumed you blokes would know Trevor by now. Moose, Joffa meet Trevor Wong, your new next-door neighbour."

"Oh, the infamous Mr Wong!" Moose squeezed his hand so tightly it left no doubt what he thought of him as they locked eyes.

Then it was Joffa's turn and he seemed to give him the same treatment.

Wong was about sixty, tall and wiry. He wasn't about to lose the first test of strength, even if his fingers were feeling crushed.

Doc Jenkins saw what was happening and broke it up with words. "Sit down here, why don't you?"

Moose took the seat next to Wong. He would have preferred to sit opposite him so he could start round two (the stare-off) but Doc Jenkins already had his bum in that seat. The Irishman rested his crutches on the corner wall and squeezed in next to Doc Jenkins, who turned and asked, "How are you feeling, Joffa? Getting some mobility back?"

He didn't wait for the answer but shifted his gaze to Moose. "Trevor's helping with some new software I'm trying out at the surgery, and we were just talking about it." He looked across to Wong. "Weren't we Trevor?"

Wong picked up his cup and swirled its contents with apparent disdain. "Best cup of coffee in town, I'm told."

"You like instant coffee then?" Moose said. "Wait till you see the breakfast? You'll think you're home in Beijing?"

"We're only here for coffee, not food," Doc said quickly.

"Do I sound Chinese to you?" Wong raised his eyebrows. "I was born in Melbourne, was raised there, studied there and made my first million there."

"So what brings you to Windy Mountain?" Joffa asked. "Besides the good coffee?"

"You know why I came here. I offered to buy the museum."

"Gus told us you and Sin came sniffing around a few weeks ago wanting to muscle in on our Bushranger Whiskers sideline."

"I have no idea what you are talking about. I don't even know anyone called Sin."

"No? So why the sudden interest in the museum?"

Wong looked over to Doc Jenkins for support. "I was looking for a place to set up my micro-chip factory. Your mayor kindly offered tax and rate concessions if we set up here."

"Maddie Northan?" Joffa looked over at Moose. "Does she even have the power to promise that?"

"Probably not," Moose said. "But she's a Northan. Like father, like daughter. The whole family is a law unto themselves."

Joffa shifted position. "So it's true. You're not building a new pub?"

"Correct." Wong shrugged. "The world moves on."

"And you say you don't know anything about Bushranger Whiskers." Joffa searched his eyes for telltale signs he was lying.

"I told you. No."

Joffa kept looking hard at him. "What about dwarfs? Know anything about them?"

Wong stared back and said slowly. "They're very little." He threw back his coffee. "Come on Doc, let's get out of here."

As they were leaving, he turned and said to no one in particular, "So, how's that vinegar working?"

————

"What's that supposed to mean?" Moose stared at the closed door.

Joffa wriggled across into the seat vacated by Doc Jenkins. "Beats me. Maybe he thinks we are having fish'n'chips for breakfast."

It took a moment for Moose to process this. "I don't think it was that. I think he was warning us in some kind of computer code way."

Joffa laughed. "Computer cod, you mean. You'd probably put vinegar on that."

"Will you take this seriously?"

Joffa dropped his voice. "Oh, I'm having very serious thoughts. But, like you, I find it very hard to think on an empty stomach."

Almost on cue, Wendy emerged from the kitchen with two plates and plonked them down.

But instead of looking down and seeing bits of egg and meat swimming in fat, what they saw were plates of oysters in shucked shells.

Moose tapped on the table. "We didn't order this, Wendy! They don't even look cooked."

Wendy stood by the table with her hands on her hips. "Everyone knows you don't cook oysters au natural."

Moose looked out the window. "That's odd. Why can't I see the Eiffel Tower out there?"

Wendy lovingly stroked the red table top. "You wouldn't find nice tables like these in France."

"But WE DIDN'T ORDER THIS MUCK! Where are our Big Breakfasts?"

"You never specified."

Moose looked up with wide-open eyes. "We've never had to specify before."

"Oysters have never been on the menu before."

"What menu? You've never even had a printed menu. You normally only offer one item. Big Breakfast. Two sausages, two pieces of bacon, two slices of black pudding, two fried eggs, swimming in grease."

Wendy pointed to one of the plates. "Nothing has changed. We still only offer one item. Today it's a dozen natural oysters. At least try them before you decide you don't like them. It's not like the stuff they used to pass off as oysters in the pub years ago." She winked at Joffa. "Good for your libido, too, love. You'll be doing Katy a favour."

Moose thumped the table, and all the cutlery, plates and empty cups jumped and rattled. "I'm not eating this muck. They look disgusting."

Wendy sighed and reached out to grab the plate in front of Moose. "Please yourself, duck, but you'll just have to go hungry then."

"Wait." Moose held the plate down. "Surely you can do me a fry-up?"

Wendy shook her head. "I've adopted a new policy. From now on, I'm only using the freshest ingredients available to me."

Moose looked down at his plate. "And these are fresh are they?"

"Gordo's mate says they come straight from the trawler."

"Gordo's mate?" Moose's voice went down.

"He sold me a potato sack of them."

"Gordo's mate!" His voice went back up again. "Got them cheap, did you?"

"He gave me a good deal, yes. He offers a good variety, too. Last week we got a bag of mussels. Can't wait for scallop season!"

"You don't think all these shellfish might be falling from the back of that trawler."

Wendy turned for the kitchen. "Look, I haven't got all day to argue. Eat them or don't. Please yourself." As she went through the saloon door, she said, "Some of us have got shucking to do."

———

Moose folded his arms as he watched Joffa spear an oyster on to his little fork and steer it towards his mouth.

"Don't tell me you're going to eat that?"

The Irishman popped in the oyster and Moose could see his jaw rise and fall as he chewed.

After he had swallowed, Joffa said, "Not bad at all. Try one."

"I think I'd rather go hungry."

"Please yourself." Quick as a flash, Joffa reached over and started scraping Moose's oysters on to his own plate.

"Hey! What are you doing?"

Joffa stopped but the last shell had enough momentum up to clatter on to his plate. "I thought you didn't want them?"

"A man can't let himself starve."

"Do you want them back now?"

"Just give me back a couple to try."

Joffa's voice dropped as he put two of the oysters back on Moose's plate. "You haven't eaten an oyster before, have you?"

"Nonsense! Back in the day I was one of the first in the queue when The Applecart served its mountain oysters."

"That reminds me. What do you think of Wong turning the old pub site into a micro-chip factory?"

Moose poked at one of his oysters, like he was trying to determine whether it was living or dead. "That place has always been a pub. When word gets out, drinkers will be outraged."

Joffa popped another oyster into his mouth and chewed. This time Moose could almost see the cogs in his head move, too, as he considered a thought.

"So do you think Wong is the one decapitating dwarfs?"

"He didn't exactly answer your question. And he has the means and the proximity. But despite what Kazza might think, it's not our problem." He tapped his finger on the table. "If I have my way, once we make the fucking concrete dwarf and hand it over, that'll be the end of any contact with the Le Blancs. Let the police sort it out."

Moose suspiciously examined the oyster now on his fork. "I don't know if he's the one trying to muscle in on the Bushranger Whiskers business though. That *is* our problem. Maybe he's a good actor but he was pretty convincing when he said he doesn't know Sin and he knows nothing about our little sideline. So it's got me puzzled."

Joffa popped another oyster in his mouth, chewed and swallowed. "But Katy said Gus said both he and Sin came to see him trying to muscle in on the business."

"Yeah, I was thinking the same thing." Moose rotated his fork, inspecting every side of the oyster.

"You don't think Gus got it wrong?"

"Geniuses don't get things wrong!"

Joffa rolled his eyes.

Moose continued examining the oyster.

"Are you going to eat that ting? It won't kill you, you know?"

Moose looked up into his eyes. "Maybe I'm waiting to see if you cark it before I decide?"

"Do I look like someone who's about to keel over? Why don't you just be done with it? Like this?" Joffa plucked another oyster from its shell and steered the fork into his mouth.

"Do you know what that looks like from this side of the table? It reminds me of feeding time at the piggery!"

"If you don't get a move on, you'll be the little piggy who has none."

"You'd steal my only two oysters?"

"In a heartbeat! I come from a big family. The quick and the damn hungry!"

Moose closed his eyes and popped the fork in his mouth. It tasted a bit like seawater, only slimy, so who could blame him for spitting it out almost immediately, complete with dribble, all over his sole remaining shellfish? "Be my guest."

Joffa screwed up his face. "Who's the gross one now?"

Moose wiped his mouth with the back of his hand, and smiled.

"So why do you think Doc Jenkins was here with Wong?"

"He said." Moose frowned. "Wong's installing some medical software for him."

"Do you know how George Pickles died?"

"George who?"

"The fella who installed the mirror above your bed."

"That happened before I came back to live here."

"Do you know Doc Jenkins has a skeleton in his surgery?"

"So? Lots of quacks probably have skeletons?"

"His is called George."

"Christ, what are you suggesting? Doc killed him? Being a doctor and having a skeleton is not evidence of foul play!"

"No? His son is also an undertaker!"

"Those oysters might not be lethal after all, but they have surely affected your brain. Give Doc Jenkins a break. He's trying to lead a clean life now."

Moose lowered his voice. "I didn't even know he was operating in this town until Katy mentioned his name. Between you and me, Doc was the one who handed on that chess set to me all those years ago and told me to wait for further instructions from my old cellmate. But I've heard nothing and Doc has said nothing about it, so I figure whatever was so important about it isn't important any more."

"How do you think Doc Jenkins and Trevor Wong know each other?"

"How would I know? Maybe they went to school together?"

"Perhaps they met in prison, too?"

Moose smiled. "Don't you think I would have remembered Wong?"

"Maybe it was at a different prison? Where did Doc Jenkins work before he came to Risdon?"

———

Moose was holding a small plastic bag when he came in. "You were right, Kazza. Tiger Kowalski's Dancing School is a supermarket now."

He held the door for Joffa who swung past him.

The Irishman was amazed he had caught up after losing ground coming down the high street. But it helped when Moose stopped to exchange unpleasantries with Tim who was up a ladder out front.

Katy lifted her head up from the computer. "You've finally been to Roses then?"

"Had to. The corner shop is closed on Sundays. I needed to eat."

Katy frowned at him. "Wendy didn't fill you up?"

"Wendy didn't give me *anything* edible."

"That's not true," Joffa said. "She served us oysters. Moose just has unrefined tastes."

"Oysters! Wendy?" Katy frowned again. "Let me guess? They were deep fried?"

"No, natural," Joffa couldn't help letting his delight show. "They were delicious."

"They were raw." Moose pulled a face.

Katy smiled. "They're an acquired taste. But who would have thought Wendy would be the one to raise the level of cuisine in Windy Mountain? Gordo's going to have a lot to live up to when he gets out of prison."

"He's got a few years yet to work on his Michelin hats," Joffa said. "You don't get much early parole when you did what he did."

Moose started towards the stairs. "You'll have to excuse me because I have a steak to cook. Emphasis on *cook*."

Joffa called after him. "Why don't I get Dave the undertaker to cremate it for you?"

Moose's voice returned from halfway up the spiral stairs. "I have the tools, I have the technology, and I have the tomato sauce to do it myself, thanks."

Joffa rested both his crutches on a nearby chair and leant on the counter. "You'll never guess who we saw at cafe? Wong was there with Doc Jenkins discussing a software upgrade he's doing for him."

"Nooo?" Katy gasped.

Joffa nodded. "He denied all knowledge of Bushranger Whiskers though. He even said he doesn't know anyone called Sin."

Joffa shifted his stance to take the weight off his sore foot. "Get this? When I asked him if he knew anyting about dwarfs all he said was *they were very short*."

"What did Moose make of that?"

"He was too busy defending Doc Jenkins, who he says is now on the straight and narrow."

"You know what I think. Doc Jenkins has always been on the straight and narrow as long as I've known him."

"Yeah, but what about that skeleton in his office. George."

"I think George Pickles was actually buried."

"We don't know that for sure."

"No, but I'm more certain Wong is up to no good than Doc Jenkins is. Them being together was probably very innocent."

Joffa shifted position once again. "Wong did say someting that was very cryptic. As he was leaving, he asked: *So, how's that vinegar working*?"

"He said what?" Katy's face turned pale. "Moose!" she yelled to the stairs. "That steak will have to wait. This is urgent!"

————

Joffa went to the door to summon Tim.

"What is it?" the Texan called in a far-away voice that came from above.

"Katy needs your help in here."

Joffa could hear his footsteps backing down the aluminium extension ladder as he held the door ajar. When Tim appeared, his T-shirt had large patches of wetness. The back of his neck had probably been saved from the ferocity of the sun, courtesy of the way round his cap was sitting, but his red forehead was testament a broad-brimmed hat would have given him better shade.

"I got as hot as a billy goat in a pepper patch out there," he said.

"Shouldn't you be better covered up?" Katy said, as he walked towards the reception desk like the Tin Man, obviously still feeling the effects of being a shell mule.

"I didn't know it was going to be so hot up there."

Tim made eye contact with Moose, who had come downstairs reluctantly and was now slumped in a chair like a schoolboy who really wasn't that interested in whatever was going on around him.

"How far did you get with it?" Joffa was back leaning on the counter.

"I'm still at the outlining stage. It's going to be slow going without scaffolding."

Moose seemed to brighten. "Why didn't you say earlier, Awesome Sauce? I reckon we can help you with that."

"Never mind that now," Katy said. "You know we thought Sin had hacked our computer? The plot has thickened because we now have evidence it might be Wong."

The phone rang, and Katy picked up the receiver. "Windy Mountain Tasmanian Tiger, Bushranger Whiskers and Aboriginal Midden Museum. How can I help?"

Her face turned pale as she listened.

"That'll be fine," she said, though it didn't sound like it was.

As soon as she hung up, she planted her head in her folded arms on the tabletop. "They've cancelled the first bus of the day. Apparently, they had no passengers at all."

"That's too bad," Tim said. In the next breath, he said, "So what makes you think Wong is hacking us?"

"Moose and Joffa ran into him up at The Wind Tunnel. You know I told you the hacker suggested the old men try sliding vinegar under the door? Guess what he told Joffa and Moose?"

Moose smacked the side of his head. "I knew it! It made no sense at the time, but it's crystal clear now. Pig's arse Sin doesn't know Wong. He's only feeding him the information from our computer."

Tim straightened up. "If that's the case, shoot, Officer Stretch will be pissed at us."

"Why?" Katy said.

"Mr Wong might have seen everythang we've seen about the dwarf."

———

Joffa tipped the chess pieces out of the box on to the work bench. One by one, he began holding them up to the light that filtered through the grubby little window of the shed.

"You won't find anything." Moose had crept up behind him, which wasn't hard with all the noise the cement mixer outside was making. Moose's connections hadn't come through so he had *borrowed* the mixer from the work site next door. It wasn't like they were using it today and his logic was they would have locked the gate if they had been worried someone would just wheel it out of there. Now it was whining and crunching away.

Various tools hung from hooks inserted over corresponding silhouettes painted on the corkboard backing. An orange cord was wrapped around a cobweb-covered electric lawnmower that was in the same corner it had occupied for years.

"Are you helping, or not?" Moose snarled.

Joffa didn't even turn around. "I don't want to deprive you of your area of expertise." He was now shaking each piece.

Moose looked left and right. "What have you done with my crutches?"

"I left them inside. I'm seeing how I go without them. So far, so good."

"Didn't Doc Jenkins say you ought to use them for a few days?"

"Doctors! What would they know? It feels fine to me, well almost."

"So, you have no excuse for not helping me?"

Joffa turned and glared at him. "How many fellas do you need to pour concrete into a mould? Didn't I volunteer to paint it? I won't ask for your help with that."

"Don't you at least want to see how it's done?"

"Why? Are you planning to set up a dwarf production line?"

"I don't know what goes on in the pretty little head of your missus? Who knows what she'll want next?"

Joffa picked up the board and began rotating it.

Moose looked over Joffa's shoulder. "What are you even looking for?"

Joffa shook his head. "There has to be a reason Doc Jenkins gave this to you?"

Moose screwed up his face. "You don't think I didn't think the same thing back in the day. I went over and over it and found nothing. It looks like a regular chess set to me."

"When did you say he gave it to you?"

"Years ago when I worked at a building site in Launceston. He said it was a present from my old cellmate but it was just a loan. At some time, someone would contact me to take it off my hands."

"You didn't think that was strange?" The pieces were lying on the bench like a black and white crime scene, and the Irishman was holding the box up to his ear.

"You're not going to tell me you can hear the sea, too?" Moose said.

Joffa tapped on the box. "I'm listening for the telltale sound of secret compartments." Joffa turned his head. "And Doc didn't mention the chess set when you went to see him?"

"Aside from the fact I am fucking sure he came to this town to get away from the criminal element and reinvent himself, I think he's forgotten all about it."

"Ever heard of a sleeper?"

Joffa tapped on the board, which was now lying upside down. Then he put his left ear closer to the bench and tapped again. "Does that sound hollow to you?"

Moose pinched the bridge of his nose."It sounds like a chess board being tapped to me. What did you expect it to sound like? Danny Boy? We've come outside to do a job but so far I'm the only one who's doing it, for fuck's sake."

Joffa turned to face him fully. "You don't know where we can get our hands on an X-ray machine, do you?"

"You want to X-ray the chess set now! Christ almighty!"

"Do you have a better idea? It has the outside appearances of being a mere chess set but we know there must be more than meets the eye."

"X-ray! Are you crazy?"

"The alternative is we start pulling things apart."

"Oh, I see what you're doing? You think if you destroy the chess set, I can't show you up any more."

"Nonsense! Now I'm a wake-up to your dirty tricks, I'm confident I can beat you anywhere, any place. I'll even fork out for a new set if it worries you so much." He picked up the white king from the bench and weighed it in his hand. "Wood is not this heavy, so aren't you curious what's glued inside the cavity?"

"I think you'll find they're weighted with little pieces of lead."

Joffa shrugged. "Maybe. But what if he's secreted little ingots of gold in there? Or diamonds? They'd be heavy, too."

"He's not that bright."

"Wouldn't you sleep better if we found out for sure by putting it though an X-ray machine?"

Moose's eyes widened. "I wouldn't even know where to find an X-ray machine."

"Wasn't there one at your prison? We had one at the entrance."

"Oh, yes that would work. *Excuse me officer, can I just check to see if one of your inmates has secreted contraband in this chess set?*"

Joffa stroked his chin then broke into a grin. "Airports have X-ray machines."

"Know any friendly security men, do you?"

"Suppose not." Joffa rubbed his chin some more. "What about Doc Jenkins? I'm sure he'd have access to an X-ray machine?"

"You're forgetting he gave me the chess set in the first place, Einstein. If he even knows there's something inside, my guess is he doesn't even want to be reminded about it now."

———

"Where are you going, Miss Kate?" Tim sat down behind the computer and watched as she picked up her handbag and lifted the gate.

"I can't wait for the afternoon buses any longer," she said. "I want to tell Sergeant Stretch what's happened ASAP."

"Do you think that's wise?"

Katy stopped short of the door and turned. "I'd rather he heard it from us than from someone else."

"Who's going to tell him?"

Katy considered this, then reached out for the door handle. "We'll all sleep better if I tell Stretch straight away. The sooner he knows, the sooner he can arrest Wong and the sooner we can get back control of our own computer."

As she went through the door, she heard Tim cry: "But what about the buses . . . ?"

———

The first thing Katy saw when she approached the new Windy Mountain Police Station was the Four Wheel Drive was missing from the driveway.

She ought to have twigged right away.

But the penny only dropped when she had climbed the six concrete steps and walked around the back of the renovated sandstone building to where the police office was situated and saw the 'Gone Fishing' sign hanging from the doorknob.

The station might be new but those oil stains in the driveway weren't. The black puddles had always set Oodles ranting how young blokes didn't know how to look after their cars any more, though he never stopped grumbling long enough to consider Stretch was no longer a young bloke. To compound things, Oodles was the one who had introduced fly-fishing to the policeman in the first place, which he had taken to with gusto when his wife left him.

But Elaine had moved back after almost a year of separation and the promise of a fresh new environment, and for some months Stretch had foregone fishing and spent the day with her, happy to keep an unofficial eye on the town while his two constables had rostered days off.

But Katy guessed the magic had worn off again, just as the snowy crusts on the Bing Bong Mountain streams had probably all melted now it was summer.

Katy hovered at the doorstep and considered her options.

Stretch and his wife lived in the flat at the front of the building, and chances were Elaine would be there. She knew she was no churchgoer, both her parents had passed on, and the marriage had resulted in no children. So there was no where she had to go.

Was there any point knocking on her door though? Stretch would be angry enough without Elaine being brought into the loop, too.

Then again, if she kept the conversation vague enough Stretch would know she had at least tried to tell him at the earliest opportunity.

She headed around to the front of the house and rang the doorbell.

Elaine seemed surprised when she opened the door. "Katy? Everything all right?"

"Fine, Elaine. Stretch has gone fishing, eh?"

Elaine nodded. Katy could hear the TV set on in the background, as well as the whirr of a cooling fan.

"You want to leave a message for him? He'll be back tonight."

"Hmm. Just tell him I need to see him."

Elaine examined her face. "You look poorly, Katy. Why don't you come in for a cuppa and tell me what's wrong?"

———

Afternoon shadows were falling when Katy returned to the museum. Two of those shadows were coming from Moose and Joffa who were carrying scaffolding tubes from next door and dropping them into a pile at the front of the museum.

"What are you doing?" Katy said when she pulled up in front of Moose.

"A bit of payback." Moose wiped his forehead with the back of his forearm, rather than with one of the dusty leather gloves he was wearing. "This will send a message to Wong that he shouldn't mess with us."

"But it's theft?" She watched through the wire fence as her husband picked up another tube next door and hoisted it on to his shoulder. He limped through the wide-open gate and turned this way.

"Who's going to complain?" Moose picked up one end of a concrete-splattered galvanised steel tube and pointed out the branding. "See this? This stencil is from no company around here. I bet someone doesn't know where this lot has disappeared to."

Katy pointed up the road with a trembling hand. "Do you know who I've just been to see?"

"Let me guess. The old couple with the gnomes AGAIN."

"As a matter of fact, no. I've been to see Sergeant Stretch."

Moose smiled. "How is Sergeant Knobhead?"

"He wasn't there actually. He's gone fishing."

"Has he? Staying home on Sundays hasn't lasted long for him. I can't blame Elaine for pushing him out the door though. She probably agrees with me he's a knobhead."

Katy put a finger to her lips. "Shhh! You want someone to hear you?"

"Stretch's going to hear me up at a trout stream near the top of Bing Bong Mountain, is he? Even if could hear me, what's he going to do? Charge me for calling him a knobhead? Isn't truth a legal defence?"

Joffa threw down his load and mopped his brow with the bottom of his shirt. He was also wearing workmen's gloves.

"Not using your crutches, Joffa?" Katy asked.

He shook his head. "I don't think I need them any more. I don't want Big Jake thinking I'm some kind of cripple."

Moose caught his eye. "You didn't tell me you've managed to track him down?"

"That's because I haven't. But I'm getting closer, leaving messages for him all over the country." He held Moose's gaze. "I've ascertained Big Jake is not in jail at the moment, and a friend I called has a friend who knows whose couch Big Jake is sleeping on. So it's only a matter of time before he'll be on the first plane over here."

"Oh, that sounds promising then," Moose said. "You'll forgive me for not holding my breath though?"

"I thought you guys were making the dwarf this afternoon?" Katy said.

Joffa put his hands on his hips: "We poured the concrete but there's nothing to do until it dries."

"Excuse me?" Moose said. "Who poured the concrete?"

"I never said you didn't," Joffa said.

"You said *we*."

"If it makes you feel better *we* can paint the dwarf, too."

"Pig's arse. You can do that all on your own."

Katy got in quick, before Joffa could add further scorn. "Got your colours picked out?"

"Brown trousers, blue tunic, black belt, purple hat and a white beard. Like Moose's!"

Moose waved a fist at him. "You're just begging me to hit you."

Joffa started walking away. "Good thinking, whitebeard. Then who's going to help you shift this scaffolding? Tim? Now *he* really is a cripple. Good luck getting any more work out of him this afternoon."

————

"I'm so sorry, Tim." Katy saw him look up from behind the counter as soon as she came through the door. "Time just got away from me."

The answer that came back was not the one she was expecting.

"No problemo," he said. "It's always good to add to my skillset."

Katy stopped on the other side of the reception counter. "You already knew how to use the coffee machine . . ."

Tim held up a plastic bag. "Yes, but someone had to do this, too."

Katy took the bag and peered into it. "Oh, you didn't?"

Tim nodded. "Rod Whish-Willson insisted on it. None of the Elvis impersonators he brought were very keen to part with their sideburns but he is very persuasive, like his granddaddy."

Katy closed her eyes. "Elvis impersonators? Where does he find these people!"

When she opened her eyes again, Tim was shrugging. "The first mini-bus carried only three people and they seemed very unimpressed when they left, didn't even stay for tea and coffee. So far, so good. In fact, it was easy peasy. But Rod pulled into the car park about ten minutes later, and that's when the degree of difficulty ramped up."

Katy dropped her head.

"Rod insisted you had a contractural arrangment with him." He pointed to the window, beyond which Joffa and Moose could be seen waving their hands at each other. "I kept hoping you'd come walking through that door, but when the Elvises filed out of the gallery, I knew I didn't have any choice."

"But how could you when I took my scissors and razor with me in my handbag."

Tim slid open a drawer and pulled out a pair of scissors, which he brandished.

Katy pulled a face. "They're for cutting paper, Tim. They're blunt."

"They did the job. He did complain the scissors pinched him, but he was complaining before I even started. Mostly he was arguing with Rod over why he had to be the one in the barber's chair."

"How did he draw the short straw?"

Tim shrugged."Beats me. All I know is he didn't look happy when Rod whispered in his ear. And he sighed when he got in the chair."

Katy rolled her eyes. "Where were Moose and Joffa while all this was happening?"

"Outside, working. I did poke my head outside to ask them if they would help but Moose told me I was on my own. He called me sunshine."

"At least he was civil for once."

"I wouldn't have said *"you can stick it up your arse, sunshine"* was all that civil."

Katy covered her mouth with a hand.

"And another thang," Tim said. "I thought Rod would be happy I had done the business without you here. But when he ushered all the current Elvis's and the ex-Elvis out the door, he stood at the counter and held his hand out. When I slapped his hand in a high five, he called me a Yanky idiot. You believe that? Turns out he didn't want a high-five. He said he wanted to know where his envelope was. I said I didn't know anythang about any envelope. He then stormed out. You believe that?"

———

Moose didn't want to give Joffa another crack at the indoor chess crown, but it was the only way to shut the Irishman up for a while.

This is how they came to be hunched over the board that night in the lounge upstairs. Joffa had walked Katy home but he had returned unexpectedly.

He told Moose this had been his doing. He said it'd be different once he had tracked down his ex-colleague and Big Jake could camp out at the museum, but for now he considered himself to be on guard duty.

"I'm sure I'd be fine." Moose reached down and scratched his thigh slowly.

"Did you just do what I think you did?"

"What of it? I itch, I scratch, especially in my own place."

"It's what you scratched that worries me. I heard the rustling of fabric."

"It was my right thigh. OK?"

"You sure?"

"It was the *outside* of my jeans."

Joffa sniffed, spat in his palm and offered his hand. "Swear on it?"

Moose shook his head. "You must think I came down in the last shower."

"I didn't baulk at it when I had to shake your yucky hand?"

"That was different. You were asking me to swear to keeping a secret then."

"Please yourself." Joffa used the same hand to move his white king's pawn two squares.

Moose looked up at him. "You did that on purpose! Now your gob is all over that pawn, how can I ever take it?"

"If that was my plan, don't you think I would have touched my queen?"

"I don't want you touching this chess set at all."

Joffa frowned. "At all? How am I expected to move the pieces then? Telepathically?"

"You tell me what pieces you want moved where, and I'll move them. Except that pawn! Leave that where it is."

Joffa locked eyes. "Are you serious? The touch move rule was a new concept for you, but now you want to touch *my* pieces, too."

Moose tapped the board. "This chess set probably cost a lot of money. I don't want you ruining it."

"It was probably stolen."

"You don't know that."

"I know it's your move. Good game is a fast game."

Moose glanced down at the board and growled. "I didn't know you were in a hurry to go anywhere? But be my guest if you want to leave."

Joffa waggled a finger. "Tempting. I have a very good book to read. But you don't get out of this that easily. You know you can lose on time in chess?"

"Bullshit!" He cocked his ear. "Like football games? Where's the siren located, smartarse?"

Joffa rolled his eyes. "In tournament chess they use clocks with flags that fall when your time is up."

"We're not playing in a fucking tournament."

Joffa pointed to a faded circular mark on the wall. "I never should have removed that clock. We could have kept time with that."

Moose followed with his eyes. "I always wondered what used to be up there."

"It was one of Billy Gumboots' tings. It was when he was dead that first time." Joffa sighed. "It's a wonder his son came out as well as he did."

"Did you hear Wash-Wish ranting today when he left the museum after all those Elvises?"

"No," Joffa said. "I must have been next door picking up tubes. What was he saying?"

"He saw me standing there catching my breath and told me I had another thing coming if I thought he'd bring us any more special customers if he wasn't going to get paid."

Joffa ran his fingers through his hair.

Moose stared. "Are we paying him?"

"I'm not."

"Kazza then?"

"You'd have to ask her."

"I get it. You two aren't talking. That's why you came back tonight."

"I came back to help you!"

"Why? I can handle anything they can throw at me."

"And if you can't, are you going to get Tim to help you?"

"No need. He can come behind and mop up their blood. Which reminds me? Why's he so quiet downstairs?"

"You know Tim. He's probably playing with his stamp collection."

Moose's eyes narrowed. "Can you even collect stamps in the era of emails?"

"You'd know, would you?"

"What are you talking about? I sent an email without any help. And it didn't need a fucking stamp."

"And look where dat's landed us."

"I dunno. We've managed to flush those rats out of the sewer into the open where we can see them. And I like what I see. A few construction workers but no sign of any of their heavies. I can take them." Moose looked down at the board. "Are you going to tell me what to move, or not?"

"It's your move, Boris! I already told you that."

The game went late into the night.

Moose finished a bishop up in the endgame.

"It's a draw," Joffa declared.

"Pig's arse. I've done enough to win on points."

"What do you think this is? A boxing match? It's a draw. Admit it. You can't checkmate me with a king and a bishop versus a king and a pawn that isn't allowed to move."

"Watch me."

So Joffa did. He watched him try. He watched Moose move his own pieces, then he watched him move the white king to where he wanted to go — and that was always dancing around the untouchable pawn.

Finally Moose spat into his palm and offered his hand. "I'll accept your offer of a draw but you'll have to shake on it."

———

Tim cursed his creaking limbs with every step in the dark. He didn't want anyone to hear him creep into the gallery and turn on the light.

Moose and Joffa were upstairs in the lounge. He couldn't hear the TV through the closed door but he'd lay odds they were watching an old western up there. Tim felt lower than a gopher hole. Moose didn't seem to care that his joints were aching because he had consigned him to another night in the sleeping bag — until the sign was actually finished.

If Moose had even suspected he was going into the gallery, he'd make a hornet look cuddly.

All Tim wanted to do was rearrange the shells in the cabinet to make sure the best ones were on display.

When he re-emerged into the dark foyer two hours later with different shells in the bucket he had taken in there, the only light in the room came from the streetlight out front and from the cracks in the back panels of the computer.

He put the red bucket down, walked over, lifted the gate and sat down in front of the screen, which came to life at the touch of the space bar.

He tried penning a test email to himself. But all the keys still seemed locked.

He looked up the email trail from the old men and saw they had responded. The vinegar, they said, had not worked.

Tim's jaw dropped when he saw the response from whoever had control of the computer.

Try sliding a saucer of milk under the door, the phantom emailer wrote. Then call out: 'Here Kitty, Kitty, Kitty.'

Even if Tim had been able to make the computer print he knew it would be too noisy. It was awfully quiet up there though he could see a shaft of light at the top of the stairs.

He knew he should somehow record the email lest it vanish overnight. Hackers often deleted files in order to cover their tracks.

A gummed notepad sat on the desk beside the computer. But where had Katy put the pens? Normally, they were bunched together in an open metal can — but he couldn't see it in the semi-darkness and didn't want to risk feeling around for it and knocking something over.

He began opening drawers quietly and trying to locate a pen by touch.

He detected no pens in the first, just a roll of tickets.

The second had none either. Hang on? What was that? Of course, the paper scissors.

The third drawer yielded a book.

He pulled it out and held it up to the glow of the computer. It was titled *What to Expect When You Are Expecting*.

EIGHT
DON'T STEP ON MY BLUE SUEDE SHOES

WHEN MOOSE and Joffa came downstairs around 6am, Tim was already dressed.

"Did you wet the bed again, Awesome Sauce?" Moose said to him at the bottom of the stairs.

"Very funny." Tim handed him the scribbled note. "Let's see if you're still laughing when you read this."

Moose squinted at the paper, which contained the scribbled words of the latest fake email. "Is this supposed to mean something? That your handwriting sucks perhaps?"

"It's my transcript of an email that was sent to Donegal in our name last night."

"Why didn't you just print it off?"

"Do I have to remind you we no longer have control of the computer?"

Moose began reading it again. When he lifted his eyes, he said," This is getting beyond a fucking joke! I think it's time we actually confronted Wong and asked him what he's playing at."

But Joffa grabbed him by a shoulder. "That's probably what he wants you to do. He just wants you to throw the first punch so he can have witnesses his construction workers were only retaliating on his behalf. Hello? Your soft head would be no match for their hard hammers."

Moose let out a long stream of breath. "Yeah, I suppose you are right for once." He waggled a finger. "But when we finish with his scaffolding, I'm going to make sure there's a few essential joints missing when we return it."

That's why they were up so early. The sooner they got the scaffolding up, the sooner Tim could finish the new sign.

"Congratulations, Joffa, by the way," Tim said as they headed for the door.

Moose and Joffa both stopped and turned around.

"What for?" Joffa said.

"Oh, like that is it?" Tim smiled. "Don't worry. Your secret is safe with me."

Joffa frowned. He gently pushed Moose towards the door. "C'mon, we have work to do while it's still cool. Tim probably wants time alone to try to nut out the problem with the computer."

Moose wasn't happy when they got to the other side. "What was that about?"

"He's obviously seen the concrete cast of the dwarf in the shed."

"I did all that, not you."

"But Tim doesn't know that."

Moose turned to go back inside and Joffa grabbed him by the arm. "Where are you going?"

"I need to set the little bugger straight on who actually deserves congratulations for making the dwarf."

"Why would you want to do that? We're like Lennon and McCartney. We share the credit regardless of who does the work."

Moose glared at him. "You're comparing us to The Beatles? Seriously? I don't recall John Lennon and Paul McCartney ever making a fucking dwarf. Which album was that on?"

"It's just an analogy, OK?"

Moose tried to break free. "I also need to ask Awesome Sauce what the fuck he was doing in my shed without permission."

Joffa squeezed Moose's arm tighter. "You told him the buckets were in there, remember? Besides, he's had open access to it while you were laid up. If he hadn't been for him, we probably would never have found the mould."

Joffa steered Moose towards the pile of scaffolding tubes and connectors. "This afternoon I'll lay the first coat of paint on the dwarf, and you'll be able to say you helped with that."

Both men worked feverishly to get the scaffolding up before the sun got too hot.

Moose only stopped to go inside for his morning visit to Cubicle Two, which seemed to lift his spirits.

It seemed like he had forgotten to grill Tim. By the time he climbed back up the ladder, he had barely gasped out the news that Awesome Sauce was still on square one with the computer when Katy had arrived and marvelled at how much work they had done.

Some minutes later, Sergeant Stretch had appeared below.

"What are you doing up there?" he called.

"What's it look like we are doing?" Moose muttered under his labouring breath. "Cooking?"

Joffa, who had been tightening nuts, stood up on the platform, looked down and saw the policeman in his cap. "Tim's offered to paint a new sign for us."

"What's wrong with the old one?" Stretch called back.

"Ask Kazza when you get inside," Moose bellowed.

———

Katy looked up to see Stretch remove his cap as he came through the door. He still hadn't had his hair cut.

"You wanted to see me," he said.

"Ah yes, problem." Katy looked sideways up at Tim, who had insisted she took his seat in front of the computer while he filled her in on the latest development with the bogus email trail and was now standing beside her with his hand on his sore back.

"It's not our fault, Officer," Tim said.

Stretch leant on the counter. "What isn't your fault, son?"

"Someone has hacked the museum's computer," Tim said.

Stretch scratched his head. "What exactly does that mean?"

"It means they've taken control of our keyboard."

Stretch whistled, then smiled. "Computer crime here in Windy Mountain!" He stared dreamily into the air. "Well, well, well, this is a silver lining. Not only will it put us on the map with the cyber intelligence section at HQ, now they'll feel compelled to send someone here to set up our PC."

"Sooner the better," Tim said.

Stretch studied him for several moments, trying to work out why he looked different. "Did you find your razor?"

Katy said, "Why aren't you taking this seriously, Sergeant?"

Stretch offered his mints to Katy, but only offered Tim his disapproving eye. "Look at it from my point of view," he said when he started crunching. "The big cheeses know I'm totally out of my depth on this one. So it means HQ will not only have to send someone here to set up our PC, they'll also have to give me more people if they want me to solve this crime."

"Oh, I think they will want to sort it, Officer," Tim said.

"Why do you say that?"

"The seizure of the computer is new but we have our suspicions the hacker had already installed spyware on this computer before that happened."

"Can you tell it to me in English, son?"

"It means whoever it is might have seen both the videos you played on the computer."

Stretch stood up straight like he had been zapped with an electric bolt. "The ransom videos?" he shrieked.

Tim nodded.

The policeman banged his head on the counter three times. "Why me? Why me? Why me?"

Katy caught his head in her hands when he was on the fourth downward push. The man didn't need any more brain damage.

He looked at her as if he were trying to understand why she wouldn't let him die.

"I could lose my stripes if you're right about this," he said. "Questions will be asked of me from the very top echelons: why on earth did I entrust an unclassified computer with this sensitive information?"

"You could blame the typewriter," Tim said.

"Are you trying to be smart, son?" Stretch stood up again, and looked at Tim with the mean, little eyes he had cultivated for just these occasions. "Let's have a look at your visa, see if it's still current."

"I ... I ... don't have it on me."

"Bring it to the police station within 24 hours please."

Tim looked at Katy.

"Don't you worry, Tim. Sergeant Stretch was obviously a Gestapo border guard in a previous life."

"Oh, that's charming," Stretch said. "I don't think you realise the trouble this might bring my way."

"I do sympathise, deeply. But I'm not going to let you make poor Tim your fall guy," Katy said. "He had nothing to do with this! Aren't you even going to ask us who we suspect?"

Stretch composed himself and took a notebook out of his coat pocket. He was standing so straight now, he seemed even taller than his 6 foot 3. "Go on then."

"Mr Wong next door."

Stretch's pupils dilated. "Trevor Wong?"

"You know him?"

"I know *of* him. Madam Mayor invited him to this town to set up his micro-chip business."

He coughed into his hand. "I was in Maddie's chambers the other day, as it happens. She had a few of the more prominent leaders of the community around for an informal chat because she wanted ..." He lowered his voice. "This goes no further than this room, OK?"

Then he looked at the computer. "Is it possible someone is listening to us?"

Tim shrugged.

A minute later they were all huddled in a corner on the other side of the room, bent over like football players getting their running instructions from the captain.

"I'm only telling you this because it's on a need-to-know basis," Stretch said.

Something seemed to catch his eye near the door to the gallery. "Is that red bucket supposed to be there?"

"My fault," Tim said. "I forgot to put it back."

Katy glared at him. "Does Moose even know you've been in his shed?"

"He's the one who told me the buckets were kept in there. But I didn't touch anythang, not even the dwarf."

Now Stretch glared. "What dwarf?"

Katy said quickly, "Moose and Joffa are making a new concrete dwarf for the le Blancs."

Stretch's face softened. "That's good of you to make a replacement for the one who was executed."

Katy smiled at him, and let that one go.

"As I was saying," Stretch said in a low voice. "Madam Mayor Northan has asked us to oil the wheels for Mr Wong. She reasons he is bringing both employment and dollars to the town."

"So you're not even going to question him?" Katy raised her eyebrows.

Stretch stood up to his full height again. "I didn't say that. But do you have any hard evidence it's him?"

"Moose and Joffa saw him in The Wind Tunnel and he repeated the exact words that appeared in a bogus email that was sent to the old men in Donegal when the hacker took control of the computer."

"Which was?" Stretch put pen to notebook again.

"Try vinegar," Katy said.

Stretch looked bewildered. "Try vinegar?"

"It's escalated," Tim said. "Now he's saying 'try milk.'"

"That doesn't sound like evidence to me." Stretch clicked his pen shut and put his notebook back into his pocket. "That'd get thrown out of court very smartly."

"Don't you want to know the full story?" Katy said.

"Not particularly. We've got no time to waste if that computer over there has been hacked."

"I assure you it has," Katy said.

"Any other suspicious characters?" Stretch asked.

"There's Mr Sin."

"Sin?" Katy could almost hear the cogs in Stretch's head turning. "The chap who bought the church?"

Katy's shoulders slumped. "Don't tell me Maddie has asked you to grease his wheels, too?"

"Nope, never mentioned him. So he could well be a person of interest."

Stretch headed towards the door. "If you'll excuse me, I think I need to go have a word to your neighbour."

———

Moose jabbed Joffa in the ribs.

"What did you do that for?" Joffa looked at him like he was wounded.

Moose waved his hands for shush and pointed downwards. "Look," he mouthed.

Stretch had just closed the front door behind him and was holding his cap in his left hand. Sure enough, Joffa had a good view of the bald spot.

Stretch was mesmerised by all the utes that had appeared in the car park in the short time he had been inside, not to mention the noise and activity on the building site next door — drills, hammers, the whine of a cement mixer and music that definitely wasn't Mozart.

When he remembered Joffa and Moose were working up above, he looked up abruptly. "Shouldn't you blokes be wearing safety harnesses?" he snapped.

"Ear muffs maybe," Joffa said. "But it's too late now because we're nearly done, tank goodness."

Stretch looked at his wristwatch. "When did these tradesmen arrive?"

"They only started work about five minutes ago."

"Really? I thought tradesmen are normally on the job a lot earlier."

"I think they have a bit of a commute. Accommodation is hard to find in Windy Mountain since the pub burned down. Ironic, eh?"

"It's good you don't mind them using your car park." Stretch said.

Moose growled, "Who says we don't mind?"

"Katy did when I was here on Wednesday."

"That was when we had mainly local workers. Look at the number-plates now? Wong has brought over his own workers from Victoria."

"Mr Wong, you mean? I hear he's a bonzer bloke. You ever see him on site?"

Joffa shook his head. "We saw him in The Wind Tunnel yesterday though."

"So Katy was saying."

"So she told you he's hacking our computer?" Joffa said.

"She said *someone* has taken control of it, but there is no way yet of proving who that individual might be."

"How much proof do you want, *Sergeant*?" Moose pronounced *Sergeant* like it was an unclean word. "He as good as dobbed himself in."

Stretch held his gaze. "Oh, I'm going to trust you?"

"Get over it! Even the Mayor has moved on after all these years. But the only thing that's changed for you is the size of that bald spot."

Stretch's face turned red and he plonked his cap on his head.

"We all have to make sacrifices for the greater good," Stretch continued. "The micro-chip factory will bring prosperity to the town."

"It won't do much for the museum's prosperity if our coaches can't find a parking spot," Joffa said.

"Well, everything comes to an end sometime."

"What's that supposed to mean?"

"To be frank, sooner or later people are going to cotton on the Tasmanian Tiger is never coming back and the logical conclusion is they'll start to question the continued existence of Tasmanian Tiger museums."

"You think so, eh?"

"I know so." Stretch pointed to the stripes on his left shoulder as if this enabled him to see into the future. Then he wheeled around and headed towards the church.

"You're going the wrong fucking way," Moose called after him.

———

The first two buses brought a combined eleven women and three clean-shaven men. Bad enough the computer was still blocked and Mayor Maddie Northan had given Wong her official protection, Katy's scissors were in danger of rusting shut and young Tim was acting strange.

She could do nothing but lock her fingers when the third bus of the day pulled into the car park.

But when five men with very interesting beards alighted from the passenger side, she hugged Tim, though he reciprocated awkwardly. "Told you Rod would come through!"

When a man in shorts and a bulbous nose appeared from the driver's side of the mini-bus, Katy was taken aback that it wasn't Rod Whish-Willson after all.

Big Nose was heading for the door, with the bearded men in tow.

Roger Dykes hadn't always been a driver. He had started off working with the company as a guide but seemed to be working his way down the totem pole in an attempt to find a cushier life.

He accepted the roll of tickets, then ripped them into their components and handed them to each of his passengers. Then he pointed to the gallery door and watched them go through before turning around and leaning against the counter. "Waste of time, if you ask me."

Katy scratched her head. "What makes you think that?"

"They are all psychics. But if they're as good as they pretend to be they'd know there is nothing in there worth looking at."

"You haven't seen our latest display," Tim said.

Katy looked at the door, which had now stopped swinging. "Are you sure they're psychics?"

"Can't you tell? I mean, they all look strange."

"They looked quite normal to me," Katy said. "But then what's normal? We've had a run on hairy backlines, dwarfs and Elvises."

Big Nose slouched further into the counter. "Oh yes, I forgot Rod brought a few of the Elvises here yesterday in one of the mini-buses."

Katy spoke slowly. "So what has happened to Rod? He's not off sick, is he?"

Big Nose pinched the bridge of his enormous snozzer. "Did you know he's related to that crazy old man who used to work here?"

"Didn't you know Rod is Wish-Wash's grandson?"

"I'm not a shrink, but you might be on to something about him having some kind of sickness. Mental illness has probably been handed down in the genes."

Katy frowned at him.

"The Elvis connection is why he's not on this route today. He only volunteered to drive one of the buses to their convention at Elizabeth Town." He shook his head. "You ever driven a bus with 45 Elvises harmonising to *All Shook Up* while you are trying to concentrate?"

Tim's eyes widened. "You mean there are more of them?"

"More?" Big Nose flicked a loose bit of cotton from his blue shirt. "They're here for the convention, hundreds of them. I drew the short straw last year. You get higher pay if you drive the bigger buses but you have to ask yourself if it's worth putting your mental sanity at risk."

"So Rod's on higher duties wages?" Katy said. She looked sideways at Tim. Rod mightn't have felt the need to go elsewhere if she had been watching the clock instead of unburdening her problems on Elaine yesterday. By rights, she ought to have been back here cutting whiskers and giving Wish-Wash's grandson his brown paper bag.

Big Nose turned and strolled towards the upturned cups on the table at the other side of the room. "At least you folks provide good coffee. All you can get at the convention are fizzy drinks. And good luck if you don't like peanut butter, bacon and banana sandwiches."

"Really?" Tim said. "No wonder Rod chose them over us."

Big Nose turned around and looked Tim in the eye. "If that's what all you Americans eat, it explains a thing or two."

Big Nose hadn't finished his coffee when one of the bearded psychics came out of the gallery, and whispered in his ear.

Big Nose rolled his eyes. "Looks like we have to go."

"Oh, I can't tempt you with coffee and bickies?" Katy said, directing her vision to the psychic. When she saw the terror in his eyes, she asked, "Something wrong?"

Big Nose slurped the last mouthful of coffee and slammed down his cup.

"I'm getting a bit bloody sick of this, I can tell you. This isn't the first place we've had to leave today because one of them has a feeling something bad is going to happen."

———

Katy and Tim found Moose and Joffa in the shed.

They had set up the chess board on an old apple packing box set between two stools.

The first thing she noticed was neither of them looked comfortable, high above the board, their legs splayed either side of the stools.

Then she saw the concrete dwarf standing in the corner. It was just how Joffa said it would be. Brown trousers, blue tunic, black belt, purple hat and a white beard.

"You've finished it!" she gushed.

"Not quite," Joffa said. "It needs another coat of paint."

Katy moved closer to examine it. "When's that happening?"

"Tomorrow, as long as it dries fully tonight. It's still sticky so don't touch."

She turned back around. "When can you make the swap with the le Blancs?"

"Probably Wednesday."

Moose looked up and moved from face to face. "Do you reckon we can get a bit of shush in here. I *am* trying to think, you know!"

Joffa seemed to welcome his glare when it landed on him. "Why don't you just resign, old man? MacGyver couldn't get out of the position you're in!"

"I'm no quitter." Moose looked down at the board again. He had lost his queen in a sneaky pin against the king and had since lost a bishop, too. Everyone watched him in silence as he assessed the position. Finally, he looked up at the Irishman. "Will you accept a draw?"

"You'll try anything to squib out of this?" Joffa said.

Moose stood up and clenched his fists. "Who are you calling a squib?"

Joffa remained sitting, the voice of calm. "The trouble with you is you don't know how to lose gracefully."

"Is that so?"

"The good ting is I've got witnesses this time."

Tim stepped past Katy towards the concrete dwarf, and he reached out with a finger to check how dry the paint was.

Joffa cried, "Don't touch." As he gestured, he stood up and his hands knocked the side of the packing box, which sent the remaining pieces flying to the concrete floor. The wooden pieces landed with a clunk and a clatter, some of them stopped crash-bang where they fell, others rolled to a standstill.

Now there really was silence in the shed as everyone processed what had just happened.

The only person smiling was Moose. Katy, Joffa and Tim looked in horror at the black and white carnage.

"Oh, dang," Tim said.

Moose wrapped an arm around him. "Don't feel bad, Awesome Sauce. Accidents happen."

Joffa had turned white.

"It's only a game," Moose said.

Tim pointed to the white king whose cross had snapped off in the fall to the floor. "I should have known," Tim said. "That psychic said somethang bad was going to happen."

"What psychic?" Moose said, looking at Tim for some explanation

"It was nothing," Katy said. "This is just a coincidence, surely? Roger Dykes thinks they just cry wolf a lot."

———

Joffa was still complaining when they reconvened in the foyer.

"You saw how far ahead I was?" he said to Tim. "Don't you think I should be declared the winner?"

"It's not up to me," Tim said. "I don't know what rules you agreed on with Moose?"

Moose grunted. "You only stipulated one rule, remember? *Wash your hands.*"

"I didn't know this clodhopper was going to knock over all of our pieces," Joffa said.

Moose looked down on Tim. "Don't you listen to him, cobber." Then he glared back at Joffa. "We all saw who did the actual knocking over. The same uncoordinated Irish twat who trod on that piece of glass."

Joffa looked at Katy, as if to say: *are you going to let him say that?* But she handed him a cup of tea instead. "We have greater problems than broken chess pieces and broken egos, don't you think? Wong still has control of our computer, he might have seen the beheading video as well as sent it in the first place, he's hijacked any chance we have of a sensible conversation we had with the old men, and Sergeant Stretch doesn't even want to know."

"Bloody stupid copper," Moose said. "I wondered where he was going this morning? He was headed in the wrong direction."

"He said he was going to have a word to Sin," Katy said.

"But why?" Moose said. "Wong's our hacker, he as good as admitted it! He obviously lied when he said he didn't know Sin. I'd bet money he's sharing information with him."

Katy rolled her eyes. "Trouble is, Stretch seems to be more worried about losing the support of Maddie Northan, who seems to think Wong is going to bring jobs and money by setting up his factory here."

Moose snarled, "He's making a good start by importing his construction workers from the mainland then. How many skilled workers in micro-chips is he going to find in Windy Mountain?"

"What if Stretch finds out Sin wants to muscle in on our bushranger whiskers business?" Joffa said. "Won't that just get us into trouble, too? Seeing as it's not exactly legal anyway."

"Relax," Moose said. "Even if he does find out about it, you think he's going to pursue it very hard when he realises it's already been operating under the constabulary's nose for 30 years? I don't think so?"

He searched Joffa's eyes.

"Besides, you saw how long he was at the church? Either Sin wasn't there or it was a very short chat." He looked at Katy. "He came walking back past us not five minutes later."

"That's right," Joffa said. "He went straight past the building site, too."

Moose's nostrils flared. "So I don't think we can rely on Stretch to sort out whatever is happening."

Tim stood up from his slouch, like his sore back was suddenly healed by a surge of adrenalin. "You think we should get some guns?"

Moose stared at him. "You? With a gun? What could possibly go wrong?"

NINE
RETURN TO SENDER

Sergeant Stretch was waiting at the door when Katy arrived at the museum at 7.45 the next morning.

"I'm afraid I'm here on official business," he said before she even had the chance to say good morning or ask him if he knew a bird had pooped on his shoulder.

"You've made some progress with your investigation?"

"Something else has come to my attention." He tapped the scaffolding beside him, which made a twanging sound and then a yelping sound.

"Careful down there," Tim yelled. "I don't know how steady this platform is."

Katy looked up. Tim was working away on the sign with a brush and a tin of paint, which explained those white spots on Stretch's shoulder.

Stretch obviously hadn't known he was up there until he looked up now and saw the young Texan with his backwards baseball cap. "You should have said something, son? I've been standing here for a good ten bloody minutes."

"I didn't know it was you down there, Officer, honest. I did hear footsteps but I assumed they belonged to Moose or Joffa."

"It doesn't matter because you're going to have to come down. It has come to my attention this scaffolding might very well be stolen property."

Katy put a hand to her face in feigned surprise. "Wong told you that?"

Stretch looked blankly back to her. "What makes you think that? I got an alert on the computer yesterday afternoon asking all stations to be on the lookout for scaffolding that went missing from a building site in Victoria two weeks ago."

Katy looked him in the eye. "The computer is all set up? You were right about your HQ swinging into action!"

Stretch held her gaze. "Why do I even need HQ when we now have a computer expert in this town?"

Katy glanced upwards.

"Not Tim. He's a foreigner. Trevor Wong came to see me, and one thing led to another."

Katy pointed to the construction site, which was still empty. "That Wong? Why would you put your trust in him when you know fine well he's the one hacking our computer?"

"I don't know anything of the sort. All I know is he comes highly recommended by Madam Mayor, and when he asked if I needed help making our network secure I gladly accepted the offer. Now he has the computer doing the job it's supposed to do." He tapped the side of his nose. "As soon as I saw the alert, I remembered where I had seen a suspicious character working with scaffolding in Windy Mountain."

"And how was Moose supposed to have transported this stolen scaffolding from the mainland? He's been here in Windy Mountain for weeks, no months."

Stretch waved a finger. "But you can't say that for sure, can you? Didn't he go away for a couple of days? A quick trip to Victoria perhaps?"

"He went to Bing Bong Mountain." She looked up for collaboration. "Didn't he Tim?"

"That's right, Officer. It's where we found all the sea-shells."

"Sea-shells?" Stretch shaded his eyes with a hand as he looked up. "On the mountain? I'm not sure that alibi would stand up in court!"

"Well, it's the truth. Moose told me I couldn't come down until I've finished painting the sign."

"I don't care what that good-for-nothing has told you. I need you to come down here now so I can get up there to check the stencilling for a match."

"I can't do that, Officer."

"Are you disobeying my instructions, son? Seeing as you didn't present your visa to the police station as I asked, I now have reason to believe you are not only Moose's accomplice, you could very well be an illegal alien. SO COME DOWN NOW before you get in even deeper."

"But, sir, you don't understand? I *can't* come down. Moose has taken the ladder away."

Stretch looked around.

"That's it! Where is he? I've got him this time! Theft! Exploitation of an illegal alien! This time I'm throwing the book at Moose! Where is he? Where is that bloody ladder?"

Katy strained her eyes to see through the glass. "He doesn't appear to be in the foyer." She went to the door, opened it and called out, but there was no answer. Stretch followed her around to the shed but all they saw there was the painted dwarf and the now-packed up chess set, but neither Moose, nor Joffa, nor the ladder.

"I don't know where either of them have gone," Katy said. "Perhaps they've gone to The Wind Tunnel for breakfast?"

She turned around and Stretch had gone.

She went out front and saw the back of him striding up the High Street towards the town centre.

She didn't know how Moose was going to get out of this one but there was nothing she could do about it.

"You all right up there, Tim?" Katy said. "Do you have water?"

"Now I know why Moose insisted I bring a big bottle up. And an empty bottle, too. He always intended removing the ladder. That guy is crooked as a dog's hind leg."

Katy went to the letter box and unlocked it.

Inside she found a sealed envelope addressed to Moose in a neat Cord Cursive handwriting.

She examined it as she walked towards the door. The envelope had no stamp, so had obviously been hand-delivered. She flipped it over. The back side was blank, no return address. How odd? She looked up. "I'll come out to check on you in a while, Tim."

———

Joffa was surprised Moose wanted to eat breakfast at The Wind Tunnel again so soon.

But as soon as they walked in and he saw Gus Foot sitting there he realised the prospect of oysters wasn't the actual attraction.

Moose pulled out a chair and sat down, and Joffa sat down next to him.

Gus nodded at them in turn. "How can I help you gents?"

"Thanks for coming, Gus." Moose scratched his stubble, which was looking more like a beard every day.

Gus shifted in his chair. "Blokes like Sin and Wright never take no for an answer. But as I told Katy, you've only got to say the word and I'll flood this town with dozens of bikers."

Joffa squinted at him. "What did you just say?"

"I said I'll flood this town with dozens of bikers."

"No, before that? You said Sin and *Wright*. Don't you mean Sin and *Wong*?"

"No, Wright. I never forget a face. They came to see me." He turned to Moose. "You remember Tony Wright? Little bloke with glasses? He did a stretch in Risdon for fraud but he buggered off back to the mainland when he got out."

Moose gazed into the middle-distance. "Yeah, I do remember him. We had two blokes inside with similar names. Whitey and Wrighty. It confused the hell out of most of us, especially Whitey."

"Whitey's still inside, isn't he?" Gus said.

"He'll be lucky to still be alive when he gets his freedom," Moose said.

"You know Wrighty broke parole? It hasn't stopped him coming back to Tasmania from time to time, mind you — but if the wallopers catch up to him, guess where he'll be going back to?"

"No wonder he wanted in on the bushranger whiskers business then. Fraud being his choice of crime!"

"That's the puzzling thing," Gus said. "The word around the traps is he's reinvented himself. Apparently, he's into computer crime these days."

They all looked up when the kitchen door swung open.

Out came Wendy with a notebook in her hand and a pencil behind her ear. "Three rounds of Cream of Mussel Soup, fellas?"

Gus looked up at her. "What happened to the oysters you had?"

"All gone," she said. "But my vendor was doing a good deal on mussels this morning."

Gus looked at his watch. "Christ, he must have been by early?"

"He likes to make deliveries in the dark."

"Oh, I see," Gus said. "Old mate of Gordo's, is he?"

Wendy put her hands on her hips. "I don't hear any thanks for me going to the trouble of putting a gourmet feast on the menu? You don't have to have it."

"In that case," Moose said quickly. "I'll have the greasy breakfast."

"Nice try," Wendy said. Her hair colour had changed so many times over the years, no one could remember her original colouring. Now she wore her blonde hair up in a bob, and a few curls were dislodged as she shook her head. "Didn't I tell you the other day, I've only got one set of hands? If you don't want the mussels, all I can offer is a mug of tea or coffee."

Moose and Joffa turned their heads when the front door flung open behind them, in time to see Sergeant Stretch burst into the room, wheezing and red-faced.

"If you're here for the oysters, they're all gone," Wendy said.

"Oysters?" Stretch looked puzzled. "Why has everyone in Windy Mountain gone batty over shellfish today? The only crustaceans I'm after are sitting right there." He pointed straight at Moose, then at Joffa.

"I think you mean molluscs, sergeant," Gus said.

"I don't like being called either of them, copper!" Moose added.

"You should take a leaf out of your young American's book. He treats me with respect and calls me sir. But what goes around comes around. You don't get to choose what you're called in Risdon. Scumbag!"

Moose turned his head and glanced across the table. "Is he allowed to say that, Gus?"

The adviser picked up the fork from his place setting and examined it. "I'd say he's unwise to say it in front of witnesses."

"Who will they believe?" Stretch said. "A sworn officer of the law or two ex-cons, a former outlaw biker and a peroxide blonde whose husband is a career criminal."

Wendy turned and headed back to the kitchen. "You think I haven't got better things to …" Her voice faded as she disappeared.

"Oh deary me!" Gus said. "How to win friends and influence them! You forget we've all rehabilitated ourselves."

"This has nothing to do with you, anyway, Foetus." Stretch machine-gunned Moose and Joffa with a shaky finger. "It's you two I've come to arrest. You especially, Moose. Step outside please. I don't want any fuss."

Gus reached across the table and put downwards pressure on Moose's shoulder. "Stay right there, fellas." He looked up at Sergeant Stretch. "I'm advising my clients to say nothing unless legal counsel is present."

Stretch glared back. "Since when did you become a lawyer?"

"The law doesn't require a person to have an actual law degree to represent someone. The courts have been hearing from dumb coppers like yourself for years."

"Please yourself. All of you can come back to the station right now."

"And why would we want to do that?"

"Because I have good reason to suspect that Moose and Joffa have been in possession of stolen goods, namely the scaffolding they've erected in front of the museum."

"Do you have any proof of this accusation, sergeant?" Gus said.

"I will have — once I climb up there to verify known markings."

"And how will you achieve that?"

Stretch smiled. "You don't think I can borrow a ladder? The construction site next door has lots of ladders, and since the owner is working out of a spare room at the police station until his place is finished, how hard do you think it'll be to get permission?"

Joffa stood up. "Wong is working with you!"

Gus motioned for him to sit back down.

"So you have a warrant, sergeant?" Gus said.

"Why would I need a warrant when I have a reasonable suspicion?"

Gus let out a stream of air, and addressed Moose and Joffa. "See what I mean about coppers without a legal clue?" He looked up at Stretch. "You must know you can't trespass on to that land without the right documentation. If my memory serves me right, the district magistrate will be here on Friday. Feel free to come back in three days' time when you've secured the warrant."

The ashen-faced sergeant turned to go, but Gus stopped him. "Is that bird shit on your shoulder, Sergeant?"

Stretch rubbed the shoulder of his uniform and looked horrified when he saw the white paint had transferred to his hand.

The men laughed as the door slammed after him.

Wendy backed out of the swinging door carrying three steaming bowls of Cream Soup of Mussels, placing one before each man.

"Smells nice," Moose said. "But, Wendy, I don't think we even got around to ordering."

"Don't you worry about it, love. This is on the house. Eat up quick. That nosey copper is bound to put two and two together sooner or later. I want the evidence gone before he returns."

———

Katy looked up when Moose and Joffa came through the door like two whirling dervishes.

"You'll never guess … ?" Moose said as they came to a stop on the other side of the reception desk and saw the puzzled look on her face.

She handed him the envelope over the counter.

He frowned as he looked at it. "What's this?"

"Someone dropped it in the letter box overnight," Katy said.

Moose flipped the envelope around. "No return address, that's interesting."

Joffa smiled. "That's what my parents did to me once when they didn't want me to know where they had moved to."

Moose eyeballed him. "You insensitive bastard! I know exactly where both my folks are. Cornelian Bay Cemetery."

Katy watched the colour drain from Joffa's face, and no one said anything until the Irishman said solemnly, "Sorry, Moose, I didn't realise they had both passed."

Moose burst into laughter and prodded Joffa in the sternum. "You should have seen your face? Priceless!"

Joffa smiled now, too. "So they're not dead?"

"Hard to tell. They stopped visiting me last time I was in Risdon. I went to their house when I got out, but a stranger opened the door and he didn't know where they had moved to."

"Are you going to open that envelope, or not?" Katy said.

Moose looked at it again. "Depends. What if it's from a secret admirer?"

"What did Wendy feed you up there? Magic Mushrooms? You're hallucinating."

"Very funny, Kazza. If you must know, we had bowls of Cream of Mussel Soup."

"Mussels? Where would Wendy get mussels?"

"I don't know, but they were much nicer than the oysters she served up the other day. These were actually cooked."

"Maybe Wendy has sent you the recipe?" Joffa said, which earned him glares from both sides of the counter.

Moose turned towards the window and held the envelope up to the light.

"Do you recognise the writing?" Katy asked.

"No, but there seems to be some kind of note inside." He ripped the envelope open and extracted the paper, which had been folded into four.

Moose read the note silently, shook his head, then handed the letter back to Katy.

It was in the same Cord Cursive hand as the envelope.

Moose,

It's time.

Leave the chess set across the road (where the memorial park bench used to be) as soon as it gets dark tonight. Someone will pick it up.

Don't inform the police, come alone, leave it there and bugger off. We will be watching and will retrieve the chess set only when the coast is clear.

Katy looked up from the note. "I don't understand. Is this the same chess set you guys have been using?"

Moose had closed his eyes.

Joffa put out his hand, and she handed the note to him to read.

"What's special about this chess set?" she asked.

Joffa's lips moved as he read, then he looked up. "Nothing as far as we can tell. Doc Jenkins gave it to Moose years ago."

"Our Doc Jenkins? How? Why?"

Moose still had his eyes clenched shut.

Joffa looked sideways at Moose, then continued. "Doc Jenkins was just an intermediary. As you know, he used to work in the prison hospital — and the chess set was actually a temporary gift to Moose from one of his former cellmates."

"A temporary gift?"

"Doc Jenkins said someone would be back for it one day."

"And Moose's former cellmate is now out of jail?"

Moose seemed to come around. "I don't think so. He's in for life."

"Who then?" Katy stood up and ripped the note out of Joffa's hands and studied the writing style. "I've seen Doc Jenkins' handwriting. This looks much too neat for him."

"I'm sure Doc's not involved in the underworld any more," Moose said. "He came to Windy Mountain to get away from those bad influences."

"Why didn't you even tell me about this?"

"We never expected it to come to anything."

"But it has!"

"We weren't to know though."

"So who do you think is behind it?" Katy said. "Sin? Wong? Whoever beheaded that dwarf?"

Joffa scratched his stubble, which was also starting to look like a beard. "You'd have to be a local to know there was even a bench there once. So it has to be an insider."

"Not necessarily," Moose said, as if a lightbulb had just gone off in his head. "You heard Gus. Sin and Wrighty have both been here before. And Wrighty was inside the same time as me."

"Whoa," Katy said. "Who's Wrighty? Do we have to throw him into the mix of suspects, too?"

Moose looked at her. "Maybe we do." He turned and started walking towards the gents, pulling his phone out as he went. "You explain the mix-up, Joffa. You'll have to excuse me. I have to go to my office to make some calls."

They watched him disappear into the toilets.

———

"What's that all about?" Katy said. "One minute he's in a trance, next minute he's rushing to Cubicle Two to put his superman cape on."

"Your guess is as good as mine," Joffa said. "We ran into Gus at the cafe. Turns out he got mixed-up with the names. I told you he wasn't infallible."

"And Stretch found you, too?"

Joffa searched her eyes. "So it was *you* who told him where we were?"

"Try stopping him when he's in that mood. Last I saw him he was marching up the street looking to arrest Moose."

Joffa thumped his chest and raised his voice. "And me! He threatened to charge me, too."

"Maybe, but I think it was Moose he really wanted to nail. I imagine you were just part of the two-for-one deal."

"He didn't charge either of us, thanks to Gus. He sent Sergeant Stretch back to the police station with his tail between his legs. He told him he'd need a warrant if he wanted to inspect the scaffolding."

"But he can get one easily enough, right?"

"Gus seems to think he'll have to wait until the district magistrate gets to town on Friday — which gives us ample time for Tim to finish the sign and for us to dismantle the scaffolding and get it back on to Trevor Wong's property."

Joffa rubbed his neck. "Mind you, we already know that slippery bastard has protected status with Stretch, so he's unlikely to face charges. You know Wong is now working out of the police station?"

"Noooo?" Katy stretched out her dismay. "He only told me Wong had helped him set up his computer."

"Apparently, Stretch is letting him work out of a spare room until next door is finished."

Katy sighed. "So we've got Buckley's chance now of convincing Stretch that Wong has taken control of our computer."

Just then, an arriving email flashed across the screen.

She opened it with the mouse and saw it was from the old men.

We couldn't slide the saucer of milk under the door because there Isn't enough room.
Jimbo says he's had enough and is going in.
We'll keep you informed of developments.

————

Moose returned from the gents shaking water from his hands.

"Stop that," cried Katy, as she headed to the gate. "Can't you see you're getting the carpet all wet?"

Moose stopped, turned sideways and waved a finger towards the gents, spraying more sprinkles. "Oh, now *I'm* getting the blame for not replacing the paper towels in there? I'll kill Awesome Sauce when he comes down."

"Why don't you give that boy a break?" Katy said. "He can't do two jobs properly at once."

"He can't even do one fucking job properly at once!" Moose hollered.

Katy put a finger to her lips as she walked towards him. "Shush. You want him to hear you?"

"What's wrong with keeping him on his toes? It won't do him any harm knowing he has to lift his game."

"He's pretty good on the computer."

"Really? The one that doesn't work any more?"

"That's not exactly true. It's only the keyboard and printer that are locked. We just had another email from the old guys."

"Spare me!" Moose said, now leaning on the counter. "What's going on over there this time?"

Joffa frowned. "Are you taking the piss?"

"Just ignore him, Joffa." Then she addressed them both. "Wish-Wash reckons the milk was a no-goer, but James is sick of it anyway so he is going in."

"Figures. The Mayor has never believed Tasmanian Tigers still walk the earth, so he probably reckons he has nothing to fear." Moose sighed loudly. "If there is a God though, please let whatever *is* behind that door eat him."

"Moose!"

"You're right, Kazza. There probably isn't a God."

"You don't take any of this seriously, do you?"

"Why should I? They were the ones who started the joke. It's not our fault Wong took over our computer and has been stoking the fire with suggestions purportedly from us."

"Who did you call anyway?" Katy asked.

"Let's just say I activated the Old Boy network."

"He means crims," Joffa said.

"No kidding?" Katy tilted her head at him.

"Turns out Wrighty *is* here with Sin, but it makes sense he'd keep a low profile because he knows I'd probably recognise him."

"But they're only interested in the bushranger whiskers business?"

Moose shook his head. "I now think that is some kind of diversion. I've never seen Sin's handwriting but I'd bet you a hundred dollars it's his hand on the envelope and in the letter."

Joffa rubbed the back of his neck again. "So how does Wong fit into all this?"

"You tell me? He as good as admitted he's hacking our computer. But it makes sense to me now about Wrighty knowing about Doc giving me the chess set. He was in prison at the same time as Whitey."

"Hang on, slow down," Katy said. "Who's Whitey?"

"My old cellmate. He got away with $90,000 in a bank robbery, in which a teller died. When they caught him, they put him away for life — but the money is still out there somewhere and Wrighty must know the chess set is the key to finding it."

"But won't Whitey be angry Wrighty is double-crossing him?"

"You didn't hear me, Kazza. Whitey is locked up in a high security part of the prison. Wrighty could drop his pants, bend over and give him a brown-eye from the other side of the fence and there's nothing Whitey could do about it." He paused. "But I can."

"How?"

"I told one of my associates we're going to leave the chess set over the road at 9pm tonight and get away from there because we don't want any trouble."

"Good one!" Joffa said. "Nothing like telling your opponent what your next move is going to be, Boris. You can bet your life, Sin and Wright heard every word of that conversation."

"Oh, I'm banking on it." Moose said. "What I didn't tell them is you and I will actually leave the chess set over there at 8pm and then take up positions across the road up on the scaffolding."

"And what are we going to do? Get down and chase 'em?"

"That's exactly what we're going to do. There are only two of them and one is no bigger than a wet paper bag with four eyes."

———

Moose kept a low profile for the rest of the day. Maybe that was what old warriors did before going into battle: went upstairs and watched Rambo movies to get themselves into the right mindset.

When Katy knocked on the lounge door, he didn't even open it.

"What do you want?" he yelled.

"I just wondered if Tim can come down for a spot of lunch."

"Why? Has he finished?"

"No, not yet."

"In that case, send him up some biscuits," Moose growled. "He has a rope and bucket up there."

She'd be glad when the crooks were in jail, the scaffolding was back in a pile next door and the new sign, *Windy Mountain Tasmanian Tiger, Bushranger Whiskers and Aboriginal Midden Museum*, was revealed in all its glory.

But as the day went on, she foresaw a problem with the bushranger whiskers bit.

The three mini-buses brought only five customers for the whole day, and none of them sported any whiskers at all, and, once again, Rod Whish-Willson, did not make an appearance. Katy tried not to be despondent but at this rate the tour company could downsize to a fleet of little electric cars.

Joffa kept himself busy in the shed.

He couldn't possibly be putting the second coat of paint on the dwarf all that time. He was obviously preparing for battle, too.

———

Moose and Joffa were crossing the road with the chess set in the fading light when Awesome Sauce called out. "You haven't forgotten about me?"

Moose turned when he heard the voice. "Er, of course we haven't forgotten. Are you finished?"

"I was finished two or three hours ago, just after Katy left to go home! I'm dying to lie down. Didn't you hear me calling?"

"Hold your horses," Moose said.

He whispered to Joffa as they reached the other footpath. "Did you hear him?"

"I was in the shed out back. Jaysus, I had to put the second coat on the concrete dwarf. You have to be more careful with the second coat because there are more fiddly bits."

Moose laid the chess set down. The marks of the hacksaw were still visible on the metal stumps protruding from the slab concrete where the bench used to be.

When he stood up, Moose asked, "You were in the shed *all day?*"

"I did other things, too. Someone had to feed Gough."

"So you had time to glue the cross back on the white king?"

"What? You never asked me to do that."

"I thought it would be obvious. You did break it." Moose squinted at Joffa and gestured towards the chess set on the ground. "We haven't a clue what's special about this set? Maybe the instruction is to take it to a certain spot, lay the white king on the ground in an easterly direction and where the shadow of the cross falls at 3pm, that's where they dig."

Joffa scowled back at him. "Are you pulling my chain? Because I thought the plan was to chase them and make a citizen's arrest."

Their argument was interrupted by Awesome Sauce clearing his throat loudly. "Guys, I'm still up here."

"We're coming, we're coming," Moose said, as he turned.

The ladder was where he had left it — against the wall on the opposite side of the museum to the path that led to the shed. Moose grabbed one end, and Joffa the other and they brought it to the front.

"Are you sure you're finished, Awesome Sauce?" Moose's view of it was obscured by scaffolding.

"I've been up here all day, what do you think?"

Moose wriggled the ladder into place and as he did so he got a glimpse of part of the new sign. What did you know? It looked like Awesome Sauce had done a good job for once. Those big white letters really did stand out on the red background of the facade.

The Texan started coming down the ladder. The further he came down the redder his arms and legs became.

When he reached the bottom and turned around, Moose saw his face was as red as a cooked crayfish.

He glared at Moose. "I can't believe you left me up there for so long."

"What can I say?" Moose said. "We both got busy with other

things. But if it's any consolation to you, it's our turn up there now. Me and Joffa."

"Don't you trust me?"

Moose smiled at him. "It's not that. It's just we need to use the platform for surveillance." He pointed to the chess set lying on the concrete on the other side of the High Street. "Someone will pick that up tonight — and we want to catch them in the act."

"Really? You need help?"

"No, you've done enough today. Get yourself inside. See if there's any Aloe Vera cream in the bathroom cabinet."

"How long will you be up there?"

"Hopefully, not longer than an hour or two. The temperature drops rapidly at night."

The ladder bent and vibrated as they climbed up.

"What do we do now?" Joffa asked as they scrambled to their feet.

"We wait." Moose sat down again, his legs over the side.

Joffa stayed standing and started to read the sign. He actually read it twice. After a minute, he said, "You might want to take a look at this?"

"Yeah, Awesome Sauce has done a good job this time."

"To a point. But I really think you should read this."

Moose grabbed the safety rail and twisted himself around. He couldn't believe his eyes when he read the sign and realised it was incomplete:

WINDY MOUNTAIN TASMANIAN TIGER, BUSHRANGER WHISKERS AND ABO-

He turned around in time to see Awesome Sauce removing the ladder.

"Put that fucking ladder back up right now, or else," he bellowed.

But it was too late. Awesome Sauce already had his fingers in his ears.

"I can't hear you," he cried as he hobbled towards the door.

———

"What do we do now?" Joffa got on his hands and knees, and peered over the side. It looked a lot further down than it had up from the bottom of the ladder.

He heard Moose smack a fist into his palm above him. "We'll have to wait up here until that little rodent comes to his senses."

Joffa retreated from the edge and turned on to his side and looked up. "But what if he doesn't return the ladder?"

"Oh, he will if he knows what's good for him. I'm going to phone him right now and tell him to get his scrawny little arse out here NOW."

Moose patted his pockets, and his facial expression changed from one of white-hot anger to just white. "Fuck! I must have left it on the coffee table."

"Oh, that's just great! But if it's any consolation, I don't think he would have taken your call anyway. Did you do role reversals at your prison? If I was him I'd never want to help you down because the minute I do, I know you're going to give me an almighty hiding."

"Are you on his side?" Moose looked down on him.

"I didn't say that! I'm just playing devil's advocate." Joffa popped his head over the side again. He really wasn't comfortable with heights. He only climbed the ladder because Moose had told him to go first and pushed him on to it, but the truth was he had gone up with his eyes closed and wincing with pain every time his sore foot landed awkwardly on the rungs. Now he said, "It's too far to jump."

"We can climb down easily enough."

Joffa considered this for a moment. "What if Tim has drizzled oil over the struts?"

Moose looked at him. "Where would he get oil from? All he had were brushes and tins of paint."

"He might have asked Katy to put a bottle of oil in the bucket."

"Kazza would have said."

"She didn't say anyting to me. But then I was in the shed all day."

"You didn't talk to her at all? She didn't even come to say goodbye?"

"No, I don't know what I'm supposed to have done. Looks like I'm staying here tonight again anyway."

Moose peered over the side. Unlike Joffa, he remained on his feet and held on to the safety rail as he looked down.

"I can't see any signs of fucking oil."

"Doesn't mean it's not there." Joffa scrambled to his feet. "If you really want to try climbing down now, go for it. I'll see how you go."

"What am I? Your crash test dummy?" Moose closed his eyes and sucked in a big intake of air. He opened his eyes. "You're chicken, aren't you?"

"I'll visit you in the spinal hospital, help you with your meals if you've lost the use of your limbs."

Moose looked over the side again, then spat into the void. "You're just lucky I'm not the type of bloke to leave a mate alone up here."

"So you're staying put?"

"It won't be for long. They're bound to make the pick-up in an hour or two."

"Have you thought about your plan to chase them though? That's not going to happen if we can't get down."

"No, but we should get a positive fix on them, and we'll know where to find them."

"What if they don't go back to the church?"

Moose tapped him on the chest. "Just let me do the worrying."

One hour passed. Two hours passed. Three hours passed. Four hours passed. By midnight, it was cold up there, and it was dark and overcast.

"I can see someone." Moose was sitting with his legs dangling over the side.

Joffa was sitting further back, with his hands around his knees. "Where?"

"Coming up the footpath from the town centre."

"The opposite way from the church?"

"That doesn't mean anything. They're probably covering their tracks."

Joffa saw another problem as the silhouette picked up the chess set.

It was much taller, and much thinner than Sin. It might or might not have been wearing glasses but it looked much bigger than the average wet paper bag, too.

The silhouette carried the drop back towards the town, just as the rain started.

"Did you recognise him?" Moose said.

"Wong perhaps? He might be tall enough. But so is Doc Jenkins for that matter. You sure about him? Perhaps it was Artie Rogerson? We hadn't pegged him for a suspect but he *is* tall. And here's one from left field: what about Sergeant Stretch?"

"You'll be accusing me of it next thing."

"You have a good alibi. Mind you, if I didn't know it was you who climbed up here with me, I'd be hard pressed to recognise you in this darkness."

The two men spent the next hour screaming their lungs out for help, but any noise they made was lost in the strengthening downpour combined with the fact people had little reason to be at this end of town at night, especially on such a miserable evening.

Finally, they gave up and tried to sleep.

TEN
CRYING IN THE CHAPEL

THE GREEN UMBRELLA Katy was holding on her way to work did a good job of sheltering her from the driving rain but hindered her ability to see more than a few yards ahead.

The footpath was mined with puddles, a result of the downpour which had become heavier throughout the night, and she couldn't wait to get to the shelter beneath the scaffolding.

She only heard their cries while she was shaking the umbrella and folding it. When she stepped back and looked up, she saw two small heads with sodden hair shouting at her. "Joffa? Moose? What are you doing up there?"

"Didn't you see us waving when you were coming down the street?" Moose called. "Just put the fucking ladder up."

Katy wiped water from her eyes, and shrugged.

"You just walked past it." Joffa was pointing furiously. "There."

She looked behind her and saw the ladder lying in a puddle.

"I'll need to go find Tim to help me." She scurried inside.

The Texan was sitting behind the computer and looked up at her with a red blistered face.

"What happened to you?" Katy said.

"Ask Moose and Joffa."

She pointed out the window. "Has this got something to do with them being stuck up there in this rain?"

"Why are you angry at me, Miss Kate? I didn't make them go up there."

"Come help me get the ladder up."

Tim shook his head. "I don't think so."

"What?"

"You think I have a death-wish?" Tim stayed rooted to the computer chair. "Moose will kill me for taking the ladder away in the first place."

"*You* took the ladder away? Why?"

"They left me up there all day in the hot sun. I figured I was entitled to some payback."

"When did this happen?"

"Last night."

"Last night! They've been up there in this weather ALL NIGHT?"

"It wasn't raining when I took the ladder away."

"You must have heard the rain overnight! It was torrential."

"Nope. I slept like a baby back in my own bed."

"They're going to be furious when they come down."

Tim nodded. "Yup, Moose especially, which is why it isn't in my best interests to help you."

Katy stood with her hands on her hips. "You expect me to lift that ladder on my own."

Tim raked his hair with a hand. "Dang. I forgot you were in *that* way."

Katy looked at him. "*That* way? *What* way?"

Tim opened the drawer to his left and pulled out *What to Expect When You're Expecting*. "I think my folks referred to this when I was in the womb, too."

"Is that why you offered to make all those cups of camomile tea for me? You weren't supposed to find that book. Joffa was."

"You haven't told him?"

"He's been preoccupied."

"Are you going to tell him?"

'If you help me with the ladder.'

"I don't know. While you're wrestling with it, it might give me a chance to start running as best I can towards town. Officer Stretch will have no choice but to lock me up when I confess I really have over-stayed my visa. At least I'd be safe."

Katy frowned at him. "Your visa has really expired?"

"It doesn't matter if it has or hasn't. All that matters is that Officer Stretch will probably believe me."

"What if I can get Moose and Joffa to call a truce?"

"You can do that?"

"I can with Joffa." She rotated her hand in front of her. "Moose? We'll see."

———

Before they put up the ladder, Katy made Moose and Joffa swear not to harm a hair on Tim's head.

"You wouldn't say that, Kazza, if you could see what he's done to the sign up here." Moose added spittle to the falling raindrops.

"It's not my fault I ran out of room," Tim shouted back. "But it's an easy fix. Erect the scaffolding around the side and I'll pick up where I left off around the corner."

Once inside, Katy handed towels to Moose and Joffa and they started to dry themselves off in the foyer, all the time giving Tim the evil eye.

"Why are you looking at me like that?" Tim said.

"Like what?" Moose growled.

"Like a coyote eying a chicken dinner," Tim said.

Katy in turn eyeballed Moose. "You promised!"

"I didn't promise not to think it," Moose said.

"I'm trusting you to be alone with Tim, OK?" She turned to Joffa.

"Can you step into the gallery with me for a minute. I need to tell you something."

Joffa groaned as he rubbed the towel over his head. "What have I done now?"

———

When they emerged from the gallery, Joffa was a much happier man than the drowned rat who went in.

But the even bigger surprise was that Moose was sitting at the computer with Tim at his side.

Tim looked up with a big smile on his face. "Moose has wrested back control of the computer."

"How did you do that?" Katy said.

"No idea," Moose said. "I just hit reply to the old blokes' latest email and the keyboard began responding."

Tim looked as excited as a kid on Christmas morning, "When the computer went beep, we came around here to see what had arrived and saw it was from James Northan."

"Not Wish-Wash this time?" Joffa frowned as he leant over the counter trying to see.

"No, it was definitely from the Mayor. All he says is he's now regained control of *his* laptop and the shenanigans have to stop."

"Shenanigans?" Joffa looked from face to face. "What do you make of that?"

"I'll think about it for a minute," Katy said. "Sorry, but nature calls." She headed towards the ladies.

"She all right?" Moose asked.

"Grand, I'd say, just grand," Joffa said.

Moose flicked his head towards the gallery door. "So what was all that about? You came out smiling but I didn't think you were in there long enough for that."

"Oh, very funny," Joffa said. "If you must know, you and I can have a short sleep but we're expected to take the new dwarf to the le Blancs after lunch to make the swap."

"It doesn't take much to make you smile then."

"Dat's not all. Katy also asked me to make sure you don't kill Tim."

"Now that *is* funny. You standing up to *me*?"

"Oh, and there was one more ting. Apparently, I'm going to be a daddy!"

———

When Joffa and Moose went upstairs to hit the sack, Katy and Tim waited in the foyer for the first bus of the day to arrive.

Katy was sitting behind the computer and Tim was standing next to her folding a large piece of aluminium foil.

"You sure this is going to work?" Katy asked. "I'm sure Moose or Joffa can find a whetstone in the shed."

"Trust me, Miss Kate. This is the way we sharpen all our scissors at home."

He picked up the scissors and began snipping through the thickened foil.

When he had finished, he presented the blades for her to inspect and she pretended to run her fingers along the edge.

"That's amazing, Tim," she lied.

"You reckon the tour buses will bring someone who needs a beard trim today*?*"

Katy shrugged. "We certainly need the extra income."

"I'm sorry I seem to have put Rod's nose out of joint."

"It's my fault for losing track of time."

"Think he's gone for good?" Tim asked.

"Goodness, I hope not. The Elvis convention can't last forever."

"Hmm. You think we'll ever know what becomes of that chess set?"

Katy stared into space. "I really don't know. Joffa and Moose said they are going to sleep on it."

"Has Officer Stretch heard any more from the kidnappers?"

"If he has, he hasn't told me. I think Trevor Wong is his confidante now. And that's a real problem if he's the one behind it all in the first place."

"But I thought Mr Wong is no longer in the frame?"

"Moose and Joffa are rethinking that. It could be Sin and his invisible partner are really only interested in our bushranger whiskers business." Katy picked up the scissors again and examined them. "Mind you, at this rate they're bound to lose interest pretty soon."

"What about Doc Jenkins? Is he still a suspect?"

"Depends on who you ask? Moose stands by him. Joffa says he's still dubious."

"But what do you think?"

Katy shrugged again. "He's been my family doctor for so long, I find it hard to see him in any other context."

Their heads turned when they heard a bus pull into the muddy car park. It was another mini-bus and two women alighted, followed by Big Nose.

The women wiped their feet on the mat outside but Roger Dykes burst through the door ahead of them, leaving a trail of muddy footprints behind him.

"Bloody miserable day out there." He approached the counter with his cheque-book in his hand. "Where did this weather come from? It was summer yesterday!"

Katy shrugged. "That's Tasmania for you!"

"Tell me about it! We've lost another driver, too, which means they'll pull us in for extra shifts. Bloody young blokes with stars in their eyes! They don't stop to realise they put a strain on us older blokes with families."

Katy had a bad feeling. "Which driver have you lost?"

"Oh, you're going to like this! That young fella related to your crazy old bloke."

Katy gasped. "Rod Whish-Willson?"

"Yeah, him." He pulled out a pen from his top pocket and started writing the cheque on the counter, which Katy knew was unusual because the driver/guide on the last bus of the day usually wrote the cheque these days.

He signed it, ripped it off and handed the cheque to her. "This is it for today," he said.

"It?" She chewed the tip of a fingernail.

"Only one bus a day from now on, those are our new instructions."

"But we had a deal with Sally Hopkins."

He pointed out the gallery door to the two women, and watched them go through it. Then he turned around and took up his slumping position on the counter again.

"Where was I? Oh yes, you'll have to speak to Sally, love. But I'm not sure how far it'll get you. The word around the depot is she's about to sell the company to a national firm, which is well known for cutting costs to the bone. The axe will fall most heavily on us older blokes. Nineteen-year-olds will work for less money. No matter they have never changed a tyre in their life and wouldn't know which way to go on a one-way street without a GPS directing them!"

"So where's Rod going?" Katy asked.

"I doubt we've seen the last of him. The way these things go is he'll come crawling back for his old job when he realises the pasture really isn't greener on the other side."

"But where's he going?" Tim said.

"Going? Crazy probably. He's only agreed to be the official Elvis bus driver. His will be driving the impersonators from gig to gig around Australia."

———

Joffa was relieved to finally put the new dwarf down in the le Blancs garden. He had carried it in a bear hug all the way from the museum, he was lathered in sweat and his arms were burning.

The rain had finally stopped but the leaves on the surrounding rhododendron bushes hung low because they were still dripping with water.

"Nice drop of rain." Chalky rose from a wrought iron garden seat. "My! You've done a good job with that jolly little bloke. Which one is he?"

He didn't wait for an answer. "Can't say I'm going to miss Dog's glassy eyes following me around the garden. If it had been up to me I would have told the driver to put it back on the truck and take it back to our son. But D said we couldn't do that. She said she guessed it was more of a peace-offering than a housewarming gift."

Joffa, who was still puffing, said, "Any more messages from the people who kidnapped the other dwarf?"

"Reginald, you mean?" Chalky shook his head. "It broke our hearts when he left home and anglicised his name to Reg White. Turns out though it was a good thing because it meant he couldn't drag our good name through the mud."

He waved a nicotine yellow finger. "Then he pulls this stunt. Why? He never was too bright but why would he give us one garden ornament then take another garden ornament away? It doesn't make sense! And then to go quiet. That makes even less sense!"

Moose's face crumpled while he took this in. "You're Whitey's father?" he gasped.

Chalky fixed his rheumy eyes on him. "Don't tell me you used to know him?"

"We were cellmates."

"In Risdon?" The old man slapped the side of his own head. "Of course! That's where we've heard your name? He always talked about his big cellmate." He lowered his head and sighed. "It just seems we can't leave the past behind."

Joffa felt obliged to say. "Moose has gone straight for a lot of years now."

"Oh, I didn't mean to give offence," Chalky said. "It's just D and I moved to this town to start a new life. We didn't even tell Reginald our new address, so how he tracked us down is anybody's guess."

Joffa felt awkward, and said, "Sorry, but Katy will be expecting us.

The sooner we leave with the Tasmanian Tiger, the sooner we'll be back at the museum."

"You don't have time to stay for a cuppa? I'm sure D could rustle up some afternoon tea," Chalky said.

"No, we'd better get going," Joffa said.

Moose took the head end and Joffa took the hind end.

"Told you it was heavy," Chalky said, as they hoisted it to waist level.

"It's not that bad," Moose grunted. "Just awkward."

With no footpath at that end of town, they had no choice but to carry it on the road.

Joffa knew he had the best of the deal now.

Moose was inching backwards down Hill Street and Joffa was facing ahead as they carried the museum's new exhibit.

That was the deal Moose had struck on the way there. He said if Joffa carried the heavy concrete dwarf up the hill, he would reciprocate on the way down.

As they inched down Hill Street, Joffa was conscious of his hands being uncomfortably close to the model's shillelagh and bollocks.

"What did you make of what Chalky said?" Joffa asked between puffs.

"I should have made the connection straight away. The old man even looks like Whitey. Both of them are as ugly as a hatful of short-arse arse-holes!"

"But did you believe the story about Whitey sending them the Tasmanian Tiger on the back of the truck then stealing the dwarf?"

"Sounds like something Whitey would do." Moose inched a bit further down hill. "You'll tell me if you see a car coming?"

His eyes motioned they needed a spell, and they put the model down on the bitumen. He wiped the sweat from his brow.

"You all right?" Joffa said. "We can swap ends if you like."

"You're offering to go backwards?"

"That's not what I meant. You take the end with the bollocks and I'll take the head."

"You think I'm stupid? That's got to be the heavier end, even if they aren't retracted."

"Retracted?"

"Yeah, didn't you know? Male Tasmanian Tigers actually have a pouch right under their scrotum so they can retract their testicles."

"Why would they want to?"

Moose shrugged. "You'd have to ask a Tasmanian Tiger."

"Are you joshing me?"

"You must have known Tasmanian Tigers were marsupials?"

"Yeah, but I thought only lady marsupials had pouches."

Moose shook his head. "Tasmanian Tigers are special."

"I know you're having me on!"

"You think so, do you? Let's see how accurate this model is. Reach down under his balls and have a feel around for the pouch."

Joffa pointed a finger at Moose and waved it. "You must really think I came down in the last shower!"

———

Moose couldn't wait to put the Tasmanian Tiger down as soon as he shuffled backwards through the gallery door. He slumped over the first display cabinet he saw.

"You all right, old man," Joffa said. "You're not about to have a heart attack?"

Moose looked around. He was dripping with sweat. "I can't believe you made me walk backwards all the way!"

"You made the deal."

"I only meant the hill, not all the way down the High Street?"

"Fair's fair. You made me carry the concrete dwarf all the way there. And you said it yourself, I had the heavy end of the Tiger statue."

"Blah, blah, bloody blah ... does your generation ever stop moaning?" It was only when Moose coughed and turned his head back towards the cabinet he realised what he was looking at. He used a hand to wipe away the wetness and steam on the glass and sure enough he could see sea-shells.

"Aboriginal midden, be buggered," he said. "I should have twigged earlier. These shells are the same as the ones we saw up at The Wind Tunnel Cafe!"

He stepped aside for Joffa to see. After a moment the Irishman jabbed a finger around the glass. "Oyster, oyster, mussel, oyster, what's that little one? We didn't have those."

"No, but I bet Wendy had pippies on the menu at one point."

Joffa yelled for Katy, and she came running in with Awesome Sauce close behind.

"What's wrong?" she asked.

Moose tore off the cabinet's cardboard sign, which said the exhibits could be thousands of years old, and he scrunched it up and threw it at the American. "Try a couple of weeks old. The only good thing about not having them carbon tested is we're not a laughing stock."

"But you were with me when we found them at the entrance of that cave. How else did they get there if Aborigines didn't take them to that place thousands of years ago?"

"How do I know? All I know is we need them out. NOW!"

"Are you sure?" Katy asked, looking to Moose to Joffa.

"They look like Wendy's castaway sea-shells," the Irishman said.

Moose stared into space. "I think someone else has just taken No. 1 spot on the suspect list."

"Who?" Katy said.

"Whitey," Moose said. "It'd be just like the police to keep the news he's busted out of jail a secret for fear of stirring up public hysteria that a madman was on the loose."

Katy stepped forward and wrapped her arms around Joffa. "I'm scared."

He stroked her hair.

"You'll come home with me."

Joffa shook his head. "I'll walk you home, but I think this is the place I need to be tonight."

Moose nodded. "I need to ring Gus to see what he thinks is going on, I'll ask him to check on you."

ELEVEN
JAILHOUSE ROCK

WHEN THE MORNING light streamed through the bedroom window, Katy was relieved because it meant she didn't have to try to sleep any more.

The shower was oh so good as she rotated her head so the stream of hot water pounded on her face.

She managed half a cup of tea before pouring the other half away down the sink.

She hadn't heard from Gus, not even a phone call to ask her if she was all right. He hadn't been too happy last time he had left the flat. Perhaps he was still angry at her? Perhaps Joffa's original instincts about him were right? Perhaps the fact Gus was a business partner of her father's all those years ago counted for nothing? Perhaps Moose had just forgotten to ask him to check on her?

She looked at the clock on the wall above the table. It was 6.29am.

Damned if she was going to stay here twiddling her thumbs.

She put on her shoes, grabbed her handbag and trotted down the stairs.

She used her key to open the deadlock. The lock made a loud click that echoed in the stairwell, hopefully not loud enough to carry. Katy was mindful hers wasn't the only apartment above the shops in the High Street, and she didn't want to wake any neighbours.

She opened the door as quietly as she could and stepped on to the deserted footpath, which glistened with wetness, and had yellowy reflections of street lights. It was no longer dark but the sun wasn't yet visible in the main street.

Quietly as she could, she turned around to lock the door — and that's when she felt a tap on her shoulder.

She gasped and turned around to see a man dressed in a yellow plastic poncho.

"Gus! You gave me a fright."

"Sorry. I was just trying to be quiet."

"Where did you come from?"

He smiled. "Originally? From under a rock! But I spent the night in a doorway across the road two shopfronts up, if that's what you're asking."

"All night? In the rain and cold?"

"What can I say? I like to take the night air. But I also had an excellent view of this place."

Katy's eyes widened. "Did you see anyone?"

Gus shook his head. "They would have got more than a tap on the shoulder if they had tried to pick your lock, I can tell you."

Katy looked left and right. The street was deserted. The overnight rain had stopped, but she could still smell it.

"You could have slept on the couch."

"And lose the element of surprise?" Gus shook his head again. "I wouldn't camp out for most people but, like I said me and your old man go back a long way. Snipper would probably come back to haunt me if I let anything bad happen to you."

She touched the back of his hand. "Gus, that is so sweet."

"You didn't really think I'd leave you in the lurch?" he said.

His body stiffened. "I can feel your dad's presence right now." He cocked his ear to the air. *"What's that? You want to know what she's doing out here at this time of day?"* He looked at Katy for an answer.

"I was sick of tossing and turning, so I was going to the museum early," she said.

"Moose said that's what you'd probably do, which was another good reason for me to camp out. He didn't want you stumbling into trouble in the murky light."

"So he didn't forget to ask you?"

"Moose forget? Hardly! You don't get to go to medical school if you're vague."

Katy looked him in the eye. "Are we talking about the same Moose?"

"You didn't know? I thought you'd be old enough to remember. He dropped out of medical school to come to Windy Mountain to look for Tasmanian Tigers."

Katy kept staring. "Our Moose?"

"He'd never tell you. He has an image to maintain. People expect big blokes like us to act rough and tough, especially inside the Big House, which has shaped him a lot. But truth is in the 1990s he traded a well-to-do lifestyle for a deserted farmhouse on Blackstump Road."

'Noooo?"

Gus nodded. "Mind if I walk with you? I have a feeling Moose and Joffa might need an extra pair of fists today."

"Haven't you got your own work to do."

"I'm taking a flex day."

"I thought only people in the public service took flex days?"

"Yeah, well I'm the boss and you could say this *is* a public service."

———

As they approached the museum, Katy could see someone was waiting for them at the edge of the scaffolding.

"Your customers start queuing early?" Gus said. "Someone you know?"

As they came closer, she realised who it was.

It was a woman dressed in a red overcoat and holding something covered by a checked green and white cloth.

"Elaine?" Katy said as they crossed the empty car park. "What are you doing here at this time of the morning?"

"I thought you might like some of these, Katy." She nodded downwards towards the wicker basket.

"You've been baking at this time of the morning?"

"I can never sleep when I'm worried. Stretch was up at 3am to go to Bing Bong Mountain."

Katy frowned. "It's only Thursday."

"Oh, he's not fly-fishing. Someone saw Wendy taking a bag into the bush, and Stretch thinks she's supplying food to a wanted man."

Gus looked startled. "So Moose was right! Whitey's busted out of jail!"

Elaine frowned. "No, that wasn't the name he said."

"Don't tell me it's Gordo?"

"I'd know if it was him." Her facial expression indicated she was racking her brain. " ... Smith? Schmidt? Messy? Something like that."

Gus's eyes widened. "Not Messerschmitt?"

"That's the one," she said like she was claiming the prize at the bingo call. "Stretch thinks he's hiding out with his German Shepherd up in a cave but he comes down to the tree line to pick up his food. Stretch and his two constables were hoping to sneak up on him in the dark."

Katy felt faint. "Who's manning the police station?"

"Nice chap named Wong," Elaine said.

Gus surveyed the vicinity. "Oh shit." He grabbed Katy's arm. "We'd better get inside NOW."

———

Joffa sat bolt upright in his sleeping bag on the couch as they came through the door.

"What's going on?" he said as Gus and Katy, and a vaguely familiar middle-aged woman, burst into the foyer like they were first in line when Arnotts opened its doors for the New Year's sales.

"Quick, lock the door," Gus said, and Katy turned the lock behind her.

"You still haven't told me what's going on?" Joffa said, now holding the sleeping bag with one hand and looking at his watch. "Jaysus, look at the time!"

"You have to get up NOW," Gus said. "Messerschmitt's back."

Joffa's eyes widened. "Messerschmitt? You sure?"

Gus looked at the woman holding the basket, which was starting to radiate a mouthwatering aroma. "Elaine said Stretch and his constables went up to Bing Bong Mountain at 3am to try to flush him out of a cave he's been hiding in."

"That's got to be a good ting, surely."

"Think about it?" Gus said. "If they're not back by now, it means there has been a snag. That dog of his might have smelt them coming and he moved to higher ground? They might be the ones trapped in the cave now and he's holding them at bay with his bullets."

"He's got a gun?"

"We have to assume so," Gus said.

The woman with the basket looked suddenly alarmed. "Stretch never mentioned a gun!"

"He wouldn't want to alarm you," Gus said.

Katy glared at him "Can't you see, Gus, *you're* alarming Elaine now."

"Oh, sorry," he said. "Of course, that's only one scenario for not having brought him in yet. It's possible he's not armed at all and they are tracking him through the bush. Or vice-versa." His face changed to one of amusement. "You never see police tracking down men with vicious dogs in the movies, do you? It's normally the other way around."

"Gus!" Katy sighed and pointed to the couch. "I don't think you two have met. My husband Joffa. "She pointed to the woman holding the basket. "Sergeant Stretch's wife Elaine."

Elaine shook a clenched hand at him. "You should be ashamed of yourself choosing to camp here. A husband should be at his wife's side at a time like this."

Katy motioned for her to calm down. "It's all right, Elaine. He knows now, but he really did have to stay here last night."

Joffa gasped. "You told her before you told me?"

"Hang on." Gus looked from red face to red face. "Told her what exactly?"

Kate mumbled."I'm pregnant, Gus."

He pointed from Joffa to Elaine. "You told her before him?"

Katy looked at Joffa. "I had to tell someone. I never got the chance with you."

Joffa dropped his voice. "I'm sorry."

Gus raised his. "*You're* sorry? Christ, Katy's the one who should be saying she's sorry."

"I disagree." Elaine put her basket on a corner of the table. "A man's place ought to be supporting the future mother of his child."

"Are you serious," Gus said. "You have no idea what Joffa has been dealing with around here!" His eyes were firing fire-bolts at hers. "Come to think of it, what are you even doing here at this time of the morning."

"Simple. Katy told me she's been having problems sleeping, so where else would she be? When I arrived, I saw through the window that Irish lump was asleep on the couch."

Joffa added quickly, "I lost the toss of the coin with Moose to decide which of us would sleep down here. We couldn't pull rank on Tim this time. What's the point of putting a poodle on guard duty?"

Elaine looked darkly at him again."Typical apha male!"

With all this crossfire in the foyer, no one heard the big bus pull into the car park or saw the 40 Elvis impersonators step down.

But they turned as soon as the *Hunka, Hunka Burning Love* chorus started up.

The car park was full of glittering costumes, pouting lips, hairy chests and gyrating hips.

The driver jumped down from his side of the bus. All eyes fell on Wash-Wish, who had sideburns he never used to have.

———

Katy unlocked the door when she saw he was heading this way, then she scrambled to her post behind the computer.

"Nice jumpsuit!" Katy said when Rod Whish-Willson approached the desk with a laden cotton bag.

"Do you like the sideburns?" He flicked his head from side to side in case she couldn't see. "Don't tell the other guys but they're fake. I stuck them on myself."

Katy sighed. "That would explain why they're crooked."

"Are they?" He dabbed his hand on the left-hand side of his face. "Can you straighten them for me?"

Katy looked outside the window. "I heard you had a new job. That's not so good for us, but congratulations. "

"Thanks. This is the first stop on our tour around Australia."

"I wouldn't have thought there'd be many people wanting to hire multiple Elvises for the one show."

"You'd be surprised. Forty Elvises singing *Crying in the Chapel* at the same time is very powerful, very emotive."

Katy tossed back her hair. "Maybe, but we're going to miss you."

Rod's eyes narrowed. "Even though I have this new job, you didn't think I'd forget you, did you? I even brought you a new pair of sideburns to cut."

"Yours?"

"No, not mine. Goodness, I need to look like one of them if I want to keep this job. " He pointed out the window to an Elvis who didn't look happy like the others. "He drew the short straw on the bus."

Everyone in the room turned to look, except Joffa. Katy could see her naked husband was getting out of his sleeping bag now the focus on him had been diverted. He grabbed his clothes from a nearby chair and quickly made himself decent while she did her best to keep the conversation going. "You drew straws! So that's how you persuaded that fellow the other day to part with his sideburns."

"Oh, him?" Rod shook his head. "No, I blackmailed *him*. I got wind he was also moonlighting as a Johnny Cash impersonator so I threatened to name and shame him." He laughed. "Mind you, I hope the scissors you use today are sharper than the ones Tim used. I don't know why he had to cut some of his chest hair, too. I think some of his tears resulted from actual pain."

"It's okey dokey because I sharpened them." Everyone looked up to the young Texan coming down the stairs with an awkward gait. "Didn't I, Miss Kate?"

"Yessss," she lied again. But then she frowned. "You cut his chest hair, too?"

Following Tim down was Moose. "Can't a bloke be allowed a bit of a sleep in?" Then he noticed Gus was there too and Stretch's wife and an Elvis impersonator. Then he heard the singing outside. "For Christ's-sake, what's going on?"

Katy nodded at Rod, and the penny dropped for him. "You going to a fancy-dress party, Wash-Wish?" As he came down the last steps he inspected him more closely. "You've stuffed a sock into your grundies. For fuck's sake!"

Rod looked down. "Damn, is that not straight either?" He looked over at Katy.

"Don't look at me! I think you'll need to straighten that yourself, Rod."

"I'll have to use the gents."

"If you're looking for a good echo, Elvis, I'd recommend using Cubicle Two," Moose said.

Rod frowned his bewilderment then handed Katy the bag, which was quite heavy with coins. "We took up a collection on the bus. You can count it if you like."

"No need. I trust you, Rod. You show them into the gallery, and take a seat. I'll have your sidies straightened up in a jiffy. Then you can straighten yourself up before checking out the gallery with your new friends."

"I've already seen it, remember? I'd only give it one out of ten."

"Ah, but you haven't seen our new exhibit," Tim said. "We've got a real almost-live Tasmanian Tiger in the gallery now."

Moose growled," What Tim means, Wash-Wish, is we've got a very life-like model."

"First time I saw it, I thought it was the real thing," Tim said.

Katy spoke up before Moose's hackles were raised again. "You can decide later, Rod. How about you get your Elvises into the gallery now?"

Elaine decided this was a good time to leave. "I'm sure Mr Wong would have rung me on my mobile phone if anything was wrong, but I'd better get home just in case."

She walked over to the counter and whispered to Katy. "I'll leave the biscuits over there, dear; don't let that slob of a husband of yours eat them all."

———

Katy wondered if they had just broken the world record for the most Elvis impersonators crammed in a museum gallery at the one time.

Certainly, it was a record for the Tasmanian Tiger Museum. She couldn't recall even one Elvis being in there, let alone the 40 Rod pushed through the door.

When the foyer had emptied of quiffs and capes, Rod took a seat in her makeshift barber's chair.

"Remember? You're just straightening them," he said, as she handed him a hand-held mirror.

Moose turned to Gus. "You don't really need to be here, mate. Joffa and me can take it from here."

"You haven't heard, have you?" Gus eyeballed him. "Messerschmitt is the bloke who has been hiding in that cave. Him and his dog."

"Seriously?" Moose held his gaze, new concern on his face. "How do you know?"

"Stretch's wife said Wendy had been seen taking food to him."

Moose puffed out his cheeks. "Got to give it to Messerschmidt. He has some balls to come anywhere near this town, and risk being identified. Something really big must be attracting him!"

"Could he be the person who picked up the chess set?"

"Yes," Joffa clicked his fingers. "Of course. I knew I had seen that silhouette before!"

But Moose shook his head. "He's never even met Whitey. So how would he even know about the chess set?"

"Oh shit," Gus said, looking towards the door. "We forgot to lock it again."

The others turned to see Sin and a little man in a blue suit and black-rimmed spectacles enter the foyer.

———

"How nice to see you all," Sin said when he saw the startled faces. "It'll save us the trouble of rounding you all up." He did a double-take when he saw Rod in the chair. "Who are you supposed to be? Crooked Elvis?"

"Well, well, well," Moose said. "My intel was right. Long time no see, Wrighty."

Gus pointed from Sin to Tony Wright. "Yep, these are the blokes who came to see me."

"Quite right," Sin said, swaggering closer to them "You swallowed our story hook, line and sinker, too."

"Story?"

"You didn't really think we were interested in your tawdry bushranger whiskers sideline?" Sin was standing up close to Gus now, and it didn't seem to worry him he only came up to the knot on the investment adviser's tie. "We had much bigger fish to fry. We were doing our due diligence."

"On what?" Moose said.

Sin spun around and smiled at Moose. "On how much firepower we'd need to bring to bear to get hold of that chess set." He sighed. "Trouble is we seem to have hit a hitch, one which Whitey never anticipated."

Moose gasped. "So Whitey is involved!"

"Of course. Every master plan needs a grandmaster to move the pawns around. But it took him a long time to work out where the chess set was. When Doc Jenkins disappeared off the radar, we didn't even know who he had given it to."

"What are you talking about?" Moose thumped his own chest. "Whitey told Doc to give it to me in recognition of my prowess."

"You don't reckon he was stroking your ego, and you fell for it?" Sin smirked. "It was a security thing. He could have given it to another dozen blokes with hard-ons because they thought they were Boris Spassky. But if Whitey didn't actually know who had the chess set, how could he tell the police if they tried to squeeze him. When the time was right, all we had to do was tap Doc. Only he did a runner."

"He came to this town to get away from the likes of you," Moose said.

"You *never* get away from the likes of us." Sin paced to the counter and turned around, and hissed. "It took us a while, but we tracked him down. We paid him a little visit."

"You're lying," Moose said. "Doc would never tell!"

"He didn't. At first! But a bit of blackmail did the trick. Did you really think George Pickles was actually buried in the graveyard? He knew too much about Doc Jenkins, and Doc couldn't have a loose canon like George Pickles blabbing left, right and centre."

"Told you!" Joffa said.

Moose squeezed his eyes shut.

"We bugged your lounge room?" Sin continued. "That's how we confirmed you still had the chess set."

"OK, I'll bite," Joffa said. "What's special about it? We gave it a good working over to try to find secret panels."

Sin reached into his pocket and held a piece of paper out, which he read from. "F3 e5 g4 Qh4. We worked it out on the chess set last night. Now we have the combination to the safe where we can find the $90,000."

Tim rolled his eyes. "What did you need *that* chess set for? Any chess set would have worked."

"Oh, the brashness of youth!" Sin said. "You wouldn't say that to Whitey's face and expect to live long."

Tim turned to Moose to explain. "F3 e5 g4 Qh4 is the annotation for a sequence of moves called the Fool's Mate. In algebraic notation, each of the 64 squares are identified by a letter and a number."

Moose whistled. "All this trouble for $90,000. Really?"

"For Whitey, it's the principle that counts," Sin said. "That money has been dormant for a long time, so it's time to start the party."

"But $90,000?" Moose frowned. "You'd be lucky to raise a decent Tupperware party with that little seed money."

"Tony here is confident he can double that in one night at the Dapto dogs, aren't you Wrighty?"

Moose squinted at the man in the suit. "Greyhound racing? I thought you had gone upmarket with computer crime, Wrighty."

"Oh, he has, haven't you, Wrighty? Who do you think hacked your computer?"

"Really?" Moose said. "We thought it was Wong?"

Sin and Wright looked at each other.

"Enough chit-chat," Sin said. "If you had just had to sense to let us have the safe, we'd be halfway to Wollongong by now. But you had to steal it?"

"Safe?" Moose said. "I don't know anything about a safe." He glanced to Joffa.

"Me neither," the Irishman said. He turned to Gus, who shook his head.

"Don't lie to us," Sin said. "It was there at Whitey's folks' place yesterday morning and when we checked at 3am today it was gone."

The colour drained from Moose's face as he realised what had happened. No wonder the model of the Tasmanian Tiger had been so heavy? $90,000 of heaviness. That's why Whitey had sent the model there.

"So, where do you think this safe has gone?" he said slowly.

"You tell me? It's actually shaped like a Tasmanian Tiger. Clever, eh? Whitey had it made in Bridgewater. You'd never guess where the keypad is hidden?"

When Moose glanced over to Joffa the look on the Irishman's face told him he had twigged, too.

"How would I know where it is?" Moose tried the brusque approach. "I look for real live Tasmanian Tigers. Do I look like a bloke who collects garden ornaments?"

Sin and Wright exchanged knowing glances. "Garden ornaments? Who said anything about garden ornaments? I only mentioned it was a safe shaped like a Tasmanian Tiger with a keypad hidden in the pouch under his testicles."

Moose tried to backpedal. "Forgive me for assuming. The le Blancs are known to be big on garden ornaments — especially concrete dwarfs. Ring any bells?"

"You think we were involved in that?"

"Were you?"

"Not directly. The email exchange to the men in Ireland was entertaining to eavesdrop on though. And we did enjoy the little video show on your computer." Sin crossed his heart across his chest. "But all we're really interested in now is the whereabouts of that Tasmanian Tiger."

"I can't help you," Moose said, holding his steely stare.

"I think I can though."

All eyes turned to Elvis who, in turn, looked to Tim. "Ask him? It's the new exhibit in the gallery." He pointed to the door. "Through there."

Moose growled at him. "Why did you have to squeal?"

"Isn't it obvious? He was going to kill us if we didn't," Wash-Wish said.

Moose looked around at Gus, then at Joffa. "Are you fucking kidding? You really think these two little blokes are going to trouble *us*?"

He spoke too soon. A man and a dog came through the door.

———

"Sorry I'm late, boys," Messerschmitt rasped. "It took longer than I expected to lose those cops on the mountain."

Adolf bared his teeth as he flopped down beside his master just inside the foyer.

"Glad you could make it, Messy," Sin said. He glanced around the people in the room. "Meet the man behind the mask, the man behind the toilet roll, the man with the concrete cutter."

Now Messerschmitt bared his teeth. At 6 foot 2ish, he gave away some height to Moose, Joffa and Gus but he was all muscles and tattoos. He was never happy just beating opponents, he liked to make them suffer. There was conjecture about who had the sharpest teeth: him or Adolf?

Sin seemed to walk a foot taller. "The dwarf thing was all down to Messy. Wasn't it, Messy?"

The new arrival nodded.

"Of course, it was all Whitey's idea. Brilliant psychopath that he is. Messy has been sneaking into Risdon to visit his friend, Gordo. I'll give you three guesses who Gordo's cellmate is?"

"Whitey?" Moose gasped.

"Oh, give that man a prize," Sin said. "Whitey thought the cops here might actually get nosey if the Tasmanian Tiger was stolen first. So he hatched the plan for the dwarf to be kidnapped. He even wrote the kidnap note that Messy smuggled out of prison for him. His plan was for the kidnapping to be dismissed as the work of a sick prankster. Then when the Tasmanian Tiger vanished, they'd dismiss it as a here-we-go-again moment, and not investigate it at all. Brilliant, eh?"

Gus fixed his jaw and eyed Sin. "Big mouth there has told you where the Tasmanian Tiger model is so I reckon it's time for you to stop gabbing and do your best. The way I see it there are three of us, six if we count Awesome Sauce, Katy and Elvis. Even if you put you and Wrighty together you'd be lucky to amount to one proper-sized person. But let's be generous and pretend you're three people and a dog. I still prefer our chances."

He didn't count on the big bloke who ducked his head like Herman Munster as he came through the door.

————

"Big Jake!" Joffa cried. "You've arrived in the nick of time."

Jake stood next to Messerschmitt and the dog, and squinted. Clearly, he recognised the voice but his eyes were adjusting to the gloom of the room.

Then full recognition dawned on his face. "Joffa? What are you doing here?"

"I live here." Then the penny dropped and the Irishman tore at his hair. "You didn't get the messages I left, did you?"

Sin shook his head. "Tut, tut, tut. You should have called him directly on his mobile, like I did."

Joffa looked at Big Jake. "You have a mobile phone now? I thought you wanted to be hard to track down."

"What can I say? Crime pays, and a man's got to earn an honest living. Mr Sin bought the phone for me in case he needs to contact me." He pulled it out and held it so it buzzed and projected a shaft of light on the ceiling. "It's even got a lightsaber app, see?"

Joffa closed his eyes. Jaysus, they were in trouble now.

————

No one though counted on the sudden throng of Elvis impersonators who burst out the gallery and filled the foyer.

"You mean there are more?" Sin said, looking left and right as the din in the room became louder.

Moose shouted, "You have your reinforcements, we have ours."

Sin motioned to Wrighty. "C'mon, let's get out of here." He waggled a finger towards Moose. "Don't think we won't be back." Then he herded Messerschmitt and Big Jake towards the door.

"I don't doubt that," Moose said as he watched them exit into the car park.

"Oh, I do," Gus said. He cocked his ear. "Hear that?"

The distant drone of motorcycles grew louder and louder.

————

It's not often police return empty-handed from a manhunt and find five new detainees in the cells.

Stretch asked Wong how they got there.

Wong shrugged. "They just handed themselves in."

Stretch peered into the cell, and realised one of them was Messerschmitt, who had led him and his constables a merry chase on Bing Bong Mountain. He had no idea who the very tall man was, or the little man in the suit. But he had seen Sin around, he had even tried to question him. He knew the dog, too. That was Messerschmitt's dog Adolf. He had been up on the mountain, too, and he had assumed him and Messerschmitt were still up there somewhere.

"You can't keep us locked up in here?" Sin bellowed. "I demand to see my lawyer."

Stretch blew a stream of minty breath at him. "But you gave yourself up?"

"Only because those bikers forced us to."

Stretch turned around to Wong. "You didn't mention any bikers?"

"That's because I didn't see any. Oh, an email arrived for you. It's from Katy at the museum, detailing who all these prisoners are and what they've done."

———

Wrighty and Messerschmitt ended up being reunited with Whitey in Risdon. Sin met him for the first time.

Big Jake was extradited to his old jail in Sydney, where there were higher ceilings.

Doc Jenkins was never charged with anything. Examination of the skeleton in his surgery showed it was actually made of plastic, much to Moose's relief. It confirmed to him that Sin had just been trying to be malicious because the doctor had dared to mend his ways.

Wong was never charged with anything, though Sin had tried to implicate him, too, at the trial.

He claimed that Wong had hacked the computer at the church.

"Why would he do that?" the prosecuting barrister asked.

"Who knows? The man has all kinds of computer tricks," Sin said. "The first email we got after we bought the church purportedly came from God, saying we weren't the kind of people he wanted in His house."

From this, Moose concluded Wong was just a practical joker, who hacked computers because he could — and decided to have some fun with the old men, too. He had no way of knowing that Sin and Wright were also hacking the museum computer.

Joffa tried to put Katy's mind at rest about him being such a big baby. He hadn't come out at 10 pounds 2 ounces after all. That had been the result of one-upmanship with Moose during one of their verbal spars. They were actually both only 8 pound 5 ounce babies.

———

If you want to know how Oodles, Wish-Wash and the Mayor were getting on in Ireland while all the drama was unfolding at the museum, you're going to want to read the next book in the Windy Mountain series.

We hear a lot of talk about Ireland having leprechauns but no one ever mentions Tasmanian Tigers!

SOME WEEKS BEFORE THIS STORY BEGINS

BOOK 4 IN THE WINDY MOUNTAIN SERIES

The old men think they're flying to Ireland to trace family history and to inherit a castle. The reality is very different in Windy Mountain #4.

It seems St Patrick was so busy chasing the snakes out of Ireland, he overlooked ridding the country of Tasmanian Tigers. Or did he?

CHAPTER 1 EXCERPT:

OPTIC AND OP SHOPS

THE BELL tinkled when the man in the washed-out overalls followed his walking stick in through the door. Behind him was a big man with grey whiskers, who was wearing a red-checked shirt and loud track-suit pants.

Walter 'Goody' Moncrieff looked over the top of his glasses, then stood up. "If it isn't Clarrie Noodle? I was just reading about you!"

The frames displayed in cabinets along the walls looked like they were long overdue for a feather duster. "What can I do for you gents?" Goody walked around to the front of the reception desk. "Don't tell me you're looking for a Tasmanian Tiger *in here*!"

The man wearing the colourful, stretchy pants turned to go. "I told you this was a mistake, Oodles."

Clarrie Noodle reached up and grabbed him by the shoulder. "If you want to actually see that castle of yours, old son …"

Then he turned to the optician and blew out his cheeks. "Sorry, Goody, you haven't met my business partner." He pointed from man to man and back again. " Goody, Bert Whish-Willson; Wish-Wash, Walter Moncrieff."

Goody smiled and held out his hand. "I recognised you from the photo." He pointed behind him to the newspaper spread open on the counter.

Oodles had first come into this shop on the Slutz Plains High Street in 1972 when he had clumsily broken an arm of his reading glasses in his car door. He lived 15 minutes' drive down the hill in Windy Mountain but this was the only optical business in the district.

Oodles guessed the optician would have been in his early 30s that first time. He had had the look of a fearsome cricket fast-bowler complete with intimidating moustache and an open-neck shirt that showed a forest of dark chest hair and a gold chain around his neck.

These days, Goody had taken to wearing ties to hide the chest foliage that most likely matched the snowy white of the hair on his head.

Let's see? If Oodles was 85 now, Goody had to be in his late 70s. He wasn't just the oldest optician for miles and miles, possibly in the whole of Tasmania, he had become the town's oldest receptionist when Rosie had retired. He couldn't afford to retire himself, and he couldn't afford to replace her. So he had a bell installed above the door, which he'd hear on the rare occasion he was out in the back room consulting with a customer. Mostly, he sat at the receptionist's desk and read.

Oodles took his scratched glasses out of his bib pocket and held them up. "I need replacements, Goody. Wish-Wash needs a new prescription. He's an 83-year-old virgin."

Wish-Wash glared at Oodles. "What are you talking about?"

"Well, you've never had a pair of glasses in your life."

Wish-Wash pointed heatedly towards the window. "How can I be a flaming virgin? Tell Goody about my grandson Rod."

Goody threw a hand to the side of his head with a slap. "I *thought* I had seen someone like you before?"

Wish-Wash broke out in a smile for the first time. "You know my grandson then?"

"No, but I've seen him lots of times crossing the road. He works over at the Travel Agency. You and him, um, share a similar sense of, er, sartorial splendour."

Wish-Wash's smile grew wider. He had just bought those elasticised pants minutes before after he had seen them in the opportunity shop window two doors along. He got as excited as a boy seeing a lolly shop whenever he saw a shop selling second-hand clothes — so he insisted they check out the op shop before going to the optical shop.

Oodles had to watch him model the new trousers. They were predominantly dark green, but with orange swirls.

Wish-Wash was thrilled they felt so comfortable when most of his other trousers felt so tight, but he wanted to know how they looked. What could Oodles say? It was no worse than many of the fashion choices the lard-arse had made.

Wish-Wash had asked the attendant if the shop took trade-ins. He told him the traffic-light-red trousers he had been wearing when he came in had only had one careful owner who normally only wore them to church. Oodles knew this was bunkum. Ignoring the occasional trip to church for a funeral, places of worship were foreign territories for Wish-Wash. Oodles also knew the red slacks were already pre-loved when Wish-Wash had bought them from an op shop in another town. The attendant was having none of it either.

Wish-Wash hid the old slacks in the change-room anyway. That'd teach them, he said. Now they'd have to go to the trouble of throwing them out.

Oodles wondered what made him think his new tracky-dackies went any better with the red flannel shirt he was wearing today and the flip-flops that showed off his gnarly toenails.

Goody switched his gaze from Wish-Wash to Oodles. "How long have you been using that divining rod?"

Oodles looked around the room, wondering where the divining rod was. Only when his eyes settled on the hickory walking stick did he get the joke.

"Oh this? I've only been using it since yesterday. Doc Jenkins wants me to get used to it before we go to Donegal in three weeks' time. We both went for our medical yesterday and Jenko also reckons Wish-Wash needs long-distance glasses. I figure I need new readers. So here we are."

Goody scratched his chin. "Donnygirl? How do you spell that?"

"D.o.n.e.g.a.l. It's in Ireland." Oodles put an arm around Wish-Wash. "My mate here won a couple of air-tickets that were offered as a prize for him doing a DNA genetic est."

Goody leaned in closer and dropped his voice, like he didn't want anyone else to hear and realise he was no longer the fearless fast bowler. "I've given up on flying. The fear of crashing was bad enough, but the final straw was hearing about that bloke who had a fatal heart attack in his seat. No one knew anything was wrong with him until they tried to wake him up when the plane had landed."

"Thanks for that confidence boost, Goody." Oodles shook his head. "That story sure trumps mine. I was only worried about putting my back out again. When Madge was alive, we once flew from Singapore to London sitting up in economy, and my spine hasn't been the same since."

Wish-Wash's chest swelled, though not quite as much as his belly. "You won't have to worry about that. The good news is you can die lying down in business-class capsules these days."

Oodles gave him a dark look. "You're very sure for someone who has never been on a plane."

"Rod brought me some brochures."

Goody frowned at Wish-Wash. "You've never flown? Not even on a prop to Melbourne?"

"Nope," Oodles piped in. "Guess that makes him an extra virgin."

AUTHOR'S NOTE

THIS NOVEL HAS BEEN PROFESSIONALLY EDITED. If you've got this far my guess is you've successfully navigated the Australian spelling, slang and deliberate oddities. But typos always manage to slip through the net, so by all means let me know if something's out of order.

– *John Martin*
https://johnmartin-author.blog

MY BOOKS

Windy Mountain series

Lie of the Tiger (#1)

He's not who he says he is. Who will rescue him?

———

Blokes on a Plane (#2)

Why is the mayor speaking old English? And where has he disappeared to?

———

Whitey and the Six Dwarfs (#3)

Troupe of Elvis impersonators come to the rescue.

———

Blokes in Donegal (#4)

Three old blokes go to Ireland hoping to discover family history. The mayor had to take his great, great, great grandfather's head, didn't he!

———

Blokes in the House (#5)

How the old blokes coped with COVID quarantine (clue: the major didn't).

———

Who Knew Tasmanian Tigers Eat Apples. (#6)

Back to before the beginning. Wish-Wash leads a public revolt.

―――――

Who Knew Tiger Sharks also Eat Apples? (#7)

A character from the old days returns in an unlikely guise. It's all about comic revenge.

———

The Life and Deaths of Billy Gumboots (#8)

'His foot, my boot.'

———

Blokes Send in the Clones (#9)

Two old blokes have a crack at cloning a Tasmanian tiger.

To come:

10 — Blokes do the Block

Someone marries, someone dies. Might even be the same old bloke.

———

Funny Capers DownUnder series

The Wrong Magician (#1)

This time he has to make himself disappear.

———

Daddy's Great Escape (#2)

If Mad Bill hates people so much, why does he make it so hard for them to leave his island?

———

Escape from Mad Bill's Island (#3)

He came seeking to find out what the British were up to on the island in World War 2. He won't like the answer.

———

Standalone novels

Major B.S. comes to the end of his Rope

It all started when he rescued the wrong group of people from a prisoner-of-war camp. It just becomes worse.

———

www.ingramcontent.com/pod-product-compliance
Lightning Source LLC
Chambersburg PA
CBHW071250250626
47163CB00002B/411